Suslov's Daughter

Habib Abdulrab Sarori is a Yemeni novelist who was born in 1956. He has been a Professor of Computer Science at the National Institute of Applied Sciences in Rouen, France, since 1992. His first novel *La Reine Étripée*, written in French, was published in 1998. He has since published seven novels in Arabic, including a collection of short stories and a book of poetry. *Suslov's Daughter* is Sarori's first novel to appear in English.

HABIB ABDULRAB SARORI

Suslov's Daughter

Translated by
Elisabeth Jaquette

DARF PUBLISHERS
LONDON

Published by Darf Publishers 2017

Darf Publishers Ltd
277 West End Lane
West Hampstead
London
NW6 1QS

Suslov's Daughter
By Habib Abdulrab Sarori

First published in Arabic by Dar al-Saqi in 2014 as ابنة سوسلوف

The moral right of the author has been asserted

Edited by Alice Guthrie

Cover image by Mazher Nizar

Designed by Luke Pajak

Printed and bound in Great Britain by Clays Ltd, St Ives plc

ISBN-13: 978-1-85077-288-0
eBook ISBN: 978-1-85077-287-3

All quotations from the Qur'an are reproduced from *The Qur'an: A New
Translation* by Tarif Khalidi (Penguin Classics, 2009)

Quotes taken from *A Season in Hell* by Arthur Rimbaud, trans. Donald Revell
(Omnidawn, 2007); *No Exit and The Flies* by Jean-Paul Sartre (Pentice-Hall, 1986)

For Abdel Rahman Abdel Khaleq

'Spiritual combat is as brutal as human wars.'
– Arthur Rimbaud

'*Where were you?*
Show me. What did you write?'
I do not answer her. The night was a Bedouin
tent, the lamps a tribe,
and I, a slender sun.
Beneath me, the earth rearranges its hills
and a wanderer meets the endless road.
– Adonis

Chapter One

Post on my Facebook wall:

Place: Sheikh Othman neighbourhood, Aden

Year: 1962 (we were six)

Hero of the hour: Hassani, a real class clown, twice our age, and ten times as big

Moment of glory: he crossed the street, and one of us threw a pebble at his back. He turned around, and in perfect, melodious, religious intonation, thundered, 'Who the fuck threw that?'

A battalion of kids scurried out from every nook and cranny, and clustered around him. In one voice, and with the same religious inflection, we shouted back, 'Peace be upon him'.

Then, bursting with glee, we formed a march: fifty children winding through the streets of Sheikh Othman. Hassani led us, chanting the first part:

'Who the fuck threw that?'

And we chanted in response (to the beat of our sticks on Dano powdered milk tins, as our neighbours watched and laughed innocently):

'Peace be upon him!'

Our childhood marches borrowed their melody from a sweet religious *moulid* song that occasionally floated through the streets of Sheikh Othman on Thursday nights. But the weirdest thing was that it resurfaced (just eight years later) in revolutionary protest marches that were a far cry from the one Hassani led.

Marches of the so-called labouring masses chanted noble, romantic lines of poetry to the same tune:

With fierce insurrections, the earth rebounded
Violence, just violence, got feudalism pounded
Only through violence have revolutions exploded
Only through violence have those scum been eroded.

These marches were part of what people called the 'Seven Glorious Days'. Bedouins from the countryside attacked Aden to make its people join the revolution, claiming that Adenis were 'lagging behind, due to the culture of English colonialism.'

The only way to celebrate violence is through more violence.

And only violence can glorify revolutionary farmers in the countryside who rose up to end feudalism and nationalise our lands.

All to the beat of Mao's Cultural Revolution.

This was preceded by landmark events:

1963: Armed struggle against British colonisation begins in southern Yemen.

1967: The People's Republic of South Yemen gains independence.

1969: A coup brings the Left to power, and the People's Democratic Republic of Yemen (PDRY) is established.

Here is the question that has long haunted me:

Why didn't the labouring masses compose a more fitting melody for their fiery words, instead of using this gentle Sufi tune we had chanted behind Hassani as kids?

Their chant had but the faintest whiff of artistry; it was appallingly lazy and in shockingly bad taste.

Forty years passed before I heard the melody again. During Yemen's 'Arab Spring', I noticed a man leading marches of militiamen in nearly the same way.

His fanatic voice bellowed, 'Each time another martyr falls!' and the militants chanted in response, 'All revolutionaries gain resolve!'

Their chant didn't have the same good-natured levity that Hassani's did.

It wasn't accompanied by riotous revolutionary applause (which would have clashed with the sweet religious melody in any case).

It wasn't aimed at feudalism, or the counter-revolution.

It was a mad cry. Impassioned but tuneless. Directed against life, against humanity.

This performance was no more than a front for a culture of martyrdom and suicide bombers, a culture of self-annihilation.

Here we are, at the end of an era of scientific socialism, entering an era of immaturity, obscurantism, and self-destruction.

Intaha al-meshwar, as the great singer Abdel Halim Hafez would say: the journey is over.

One day I'll come face to face with Death himself, the Wrecker of Pleasures and Earthly Delights. If he asks me to look back on life and say a few words, I'll tell him this:

'Honestly, I don't understand anything. I'd be grateful, dear Reaper, if you'd help me grasp it all by explaining a thing or two. Surely, God has revealed to you the enigmas of creation and vicissitudes of fate, hasn't he?'

If he agrees to listen for a few minutes, I'll be obliged to set aside my life's trivial details (since the Reaper's rather busy, bless him), and go straight for its deepest mysteries. If he doesn't deign to explain these to me, I doubt I'll ever understand them, even at the end of my days.

I'll start with the blind man's shop, in the city of Aden, in the People's Democratic Republic of Yemen. This was at the height of the National Democratic Revolution in the mid-seventies, on the eve of my departure to Paris on a scholarship.

It was a small shop tucked away in our street, owned by a skinny half-blind sheikh I loved deeply.

I used to pop in every day, sit on the sacks of sugar, flour, and rice, and watch him as he moved around the shop. I was amazed that no matter what his customers asked for, he always found it on the shelf straight away. With a tarnished copper scale in his hands, he carefully weighed the flour and ghee they requested, with no need for a fully sighted assistant.

I often escaped from Aden's blazing sun into the kind shade of his dark shop. 'Uncle' Saif al-Ariqi, I called him, even though he wasn't actually my uncle. I chatted happily with him, and listened carefully to his frail voice that rattled in his throat and seemed somehow to fit the gentle dim light in his shop.

To the right of the sacks where I sat was a low door leading through to the house where Uncle Saif lived with his wife and six children. When a girl of twelve or so (about six years younger than me) went into the house with her mother, the door cracked open a couple of inches, right next to me.

Her mother, Fairuz, grew up on our street. People called her 'Aden's beauty queen'. She used to visit her old neighbourhood once or twice a week (in their government car, with their personal driver). Their family had lived in a villa in Aden's Khormaksar neighbourhood ever since her husband, Salim, had returned from studying Marxism-Leninism in Moscow and been appointed head of the Graduate School for Marxist-Leninist Sciences in Aden. (People nicknamed him 'the Party's Suslov' after Mikhail Suslov, the chief ideologue of the Soviet Communist Party at the time.)

He was a leader of the highest class – and a Don Juan of the highest class too.

Their daughter's name suited her: Faten, which means alluring. But I would prefer, dear Reaper, to call her Hawiya – the abyss.

(My name, as you know, is Imran. The name of a beautiful island not far from Aden, a place my father, Haj Abdullah Abdel Salah, loved very much. He took the entire family swimming there for a whole day every month. Most of the time we were the only ones there. Whenever I think of my father, I think of the sea. From the dawn of my childhood, he taught me to 'splash around' as he would say. In reality, we swam masterfully. Every day we went fishing together for a few hours, or took a short dip at the beach. Thanks to my father, I fell fiercely in love with the sea.

For me, it's magical, like an opiate. In it, I'm born anew. I need it instinctively, pathologically. In it, an endless wave of memories washes over me: of the warmest and most beautiful beaches in the world. At Aden's beaches, you can swim twenty-four hours a day, every day of the year.)

Whenever her mother visited our street, Hawiya came and stood by the door like a statue, barely two meters away from me. At first, she always looked at Uncle Saif and his shelves, for a long time.

I could see her peripherally, just behind the door. Then she would turn towards me, slowly. Millimetre by millimetre. Nanometer by nanometer. Until she faced me directly. Fixed her eyes on mine. Stared at me silently, innocently. Boldly. For a minute;

two minutes;

an hour;

two hours.

She would keep her laser-like gaze on me until a customer arrived. When they came into the shop, she would turn back to face the shelf and Uncle Saif until they left. Then, her gaze would return to where it had left off and burn through me again.

I'd look at Uncle Saif, and nowhere else. Only sometimes – quickly, shyly, and frustratingly – did I cast a furtive glance that skimmed across the edge of the door and passed over the young girl's face. A thin but telling ribbon of sweat traced its way down my face. I was in a state, that was clear for anyone to see. Her eyes held a smile that took pity on me, mocked my frustration, maybe.

I'd look at Uncle Saif, then back at her. Daring to stare at her for a long moment, then not daring to.

This strange, silent ritual repeated itself once or twice a week. I waited for it every day, with building desire.

'Maybe, dear Stealer of Spirits, it was that I'd never seen such a beautiful, angelic face in my whole life, and on such a promising body,' I'll whisper to Azazeel.

In the last few days before my trip from Aden to Paris, I dared to stare at Hawiya for a few minutes, sometimes, as her gaze bored through me. But we didn't utter a syllable, let alone a word. Maybe she was waiting for me to say something. I don't know.

After all, what could I say to a girl who was two thirds of my age? (I was eighteen.) A girl I couldn't possibly share my life with? Our difference in age (six years) was as insurmountable as the 'Planck Era' (in quantum theory). This wall of time, an impassable barrier imposed by the Marxist-Leninist revolutionary convictions I held back then, decreed that my life partner should be no more than five years younger or older than me.

Even so, her face never left my thoughts. Neither did her gentle, penetrating stare. She didn't often smile, but her bright, beautiful eyes were still a source of joy for me.

I remember this: there was a certain sadness in the way she looked at me, a worrying silence.

I could vaguely make out two dark crescents underneath her bright eyes. They suggested that she didn't sleep well, that at night she suffered from persistent insomnia, or deep pain.

I wonder, dear Captain of the Ship of the Dead: why did she stare at me like that? A silly game? A strange love? Did she want to divulge something? Why didn't she smile, even once?

When I slept on our roof right beneath a sky overflowing with stars, it was Hawiya's face that filled the night. Before I fell asleep, I always stared into it and told her all the things I could never say aloud when we met in the blind man's shop.

I never dared to stroke her face or kiss her, not even in my imagination. A stalwart party sergeant would appear, holding a sign with the words: *Planck Era.*

On one of our last encounters before I left to study in Paris, the game of statues ended with a silent, resounding tremor, and intense, jostling emotions. Two tears glistened in Hawiya's dark eyes, and then streamed down her face.

Two tears secretly, silently streamed down inside me too, unseen by my little sweetheart Faten – sorry, I mean Hawiya!

I promise you this, dear Breaker of Desires and Ender of Delights. In all the nights I slept on the roof of our house, staring up at Aden's starry skies, conjuring a conversation between two silent statues in the blind man's shop, I never dared to imagine holding Hawiya, or even kissing her. I didn't want to be a criminal, or violate an innocent child.

And besides, when it came to the flesh and its desires, I had
flown
straight
into
the
arms
of
Ms. Doctor.

Chapter Two

P ost on my Facebook wall:

If the Angel of Revolutions comes to me on Judgment Day and asks for a bank statement of my personal activities during the Yemeni Revolution, I'll only be able to show him three deposits from my student days in Aden, which he'll almost certainly find trivial and trifling.

Deposit No. 1:

It's 1966, a year before independence from British colonisation in 1967, and I'm ten. I greatly admire people who write inflammatory graffiti supporting armed revolution. There are slogans like: *Down with colonisation!* and phrases praising either of the two main parties vying to lead the armed struggle: the National Liberation Front and the Front for the Liberation of Occupied South Yemen.

I favour the former, though I'm not quite sure why. I support the YMCA football team over the Crescent team in Aden, cheer for Zamalek over al-Ahly when it comes to Egyptian club teams, and prefer Abdel Halim Hafez to Farid al-Atrash, but I couldn't tell you why in any of these cases.

On a pitch-black night when I'm ten, a friend and I buy a can of red paint then go and write slogans on the wall of a girl's primary school facing our alley. I write these two stanzas:

Oh great, daring liberating Front, thou hast
Made our hearts tremble; steel your determination and resiliantness
The people are with you, and your determinancy
The sun shakes hands with hope and glory!

Looking back today, they seem like broken verses, straight out of Arabic poetry's period of decadence, known for its hyperbole and frivolity. The second line of the first stanza is far too overcrowded, and there are words in the poem not found in any Arabic dictionary, like 'resiliantness' and 'determinancy'.

At any rate! I paint these lines on the wall, trembling with the fear that a Yemeni spy working with the English might see me, or that an English tank might pass by. (My face is half covered by my hood, even though the dark night itself is a more effective mask.)

These two stanzas remain on the school wall for at least two decades. Eventually, the paint fades as the cracked and crumbling wall erodes, in a dusty neighbourhood on the verge of collapse.

Side note: the school is called 7th of July 1994 Primary School. Everyone in South Yemen hates the name. It reminds them of the day the South was seized as spoils of the 1994 Yemeni Civil War, and of Sheikh al-Zindani's fatwa which permitted the victorious Northern tribes to spill South Yemeni blood.

Everyone detests the name because the victors imposed it so arrogantly. Local people wanted it to be called 'Noor Haider's School for Girls' after the school's first Adeni teacher, a sophisticated name that had nothing to do with the military. Ms. Haider was a wonderful person; as a kid I always liked her.

Deposit No. 2:

During my years of high school and National Service in the mid-seventies, I come across Cultural Workshops. These are to prepare young teenagers from Sheikh Othman to enter a new kind of vanguard party: the party of workers and peasants.

I 'attract' (as we used to say in those days) forty candidates, the best and brightest boys and girls, including my brother and sister.

For two decades, they all become Activists of the Vanguard, Marxists and Leninists of the highest class. Then later, some of them become obscurantists of the highest class, in this new era we live in today, in which darkness and destruction have triumphed.

If on Judgment Day the Angel of Revolutions' brow furrows in anger at how ineffective I was, I'll tell him: 'Spiritual combat against Darkness takes a long time. I admit I lost the battle, but I haven't given up yet.'

Deposit No. 3:

Let me preface this contribution with a plea:

'Please put in a good word for me, dear Angel of Revolutions.'

For my year of National Service, I work as a primary school teacher in Sheikh Othman. I also serve as the Second Secretary for the grassroots arm of the Yemeni Socialist Party in the schools of Sheikh Othman, al-Mansoura, and Dar Saad.

The First Secretary is an earnest, gifted teacher: Ms. K. S.

One day in Aden in the middle of the 1970s, we decide to end illiteracy among the cleaning staff in every school in our region.

(They were a shunned and marginalised section of society, mostly of black East African origin. Before the revolution, they were referred to as servants. After the revolution, they were called the lumpenproletariat.)

Ms. K graciously calls the Department of Education to request fifty copies of a book on teaching literacy.

The book is clearly a product of the revolutionary era. It features phrases like 'the revolution is led by the workers' and 'I am a revolutionary farmer', alongside a series of drawings of workers carrying hammers and spanners, and farmers pushing ploughs marked with hammers and sickles.

In the middle of the afternoon on one of the hottest days in Aden, I take a bus from Sheikh Othman to the Department of Education in the Khormaksar neighbourhood.

(Sheikh Othman was separated from the other neighbourhoods in Aden by a long road that crossed over the sea and through a nature reserve for migratory birds.)

I pay for the books out of my own pocket and take them home in a taxi, feeling happy and proud.

Then, at four in the afternoon, I take another taxi to the school where we're organising literacy classes. It's on the outskirts of Sheikh Othman, near the broad sandy beaches that lead down to the sea.

We begin, Ms. K and I, by distributing books to our students. Then at seven in the evening, we start the first lesson.

They sit before us: weary old men and women, ground down by life, living in dilapidated shacks out past Aden's outskirts. They have spent their whole lives in the filthiest channels of the universe, amidst the garbage and dirt. Their fingers haven't touched anything but palm frond brooms and bins since they were children; they don't even know how to open a book or hold a pen.

I've dreamed of this moment for ages; I feel like someone leading a pilgrimage to the House of God. After the lesson I rush off to see my friends as usual, nearly flying with joy. We have dinner in a local restaurant, and spend the evening in a cafe at the edge of the desert.

I know I'm hastening the global victory of Socialism and the defeat of capitalism!

When I get home at ten that night, there's a surprise waiting for me.

All the women we tried to teach to read are crammed into a room in our house. My mother is moving from one to the next, gently calming them down. They're crying. They beg my mother to intervene and convince me to excuse them (and the men too) from coming to these lessons, without cutting their salaries.

These lessons were my own personal initiative, so it took me some time to understand. For them, the lessons were just the whim of a bored, penniless conscript in the National Service.

I wouldn't have met the Doctor, dear Snatcher of Souls, (and it was to her my erections pointed, not Hawiya) were it not for Hamid: a good friend of mine from high school.

How I envied the free, bohemian lives of the high school students who lived in the dorms. None of them were bound to anything, while the rest of us were subjected to our conservative families' stubborn rules and restrictions.

Our high school was built in the days of the English in an attractive modern style. It was off in the desert on the outskirts of Aden, on the edge of Dar Saad, a little neighbourhood next to Sheikh Othman.

In the middle of a stretch of desert not far from our school lay Riverhemp City: 'The first secular city in history,' as the boarding school students called it.

A few of my friends from the boarding school had a daily routine: they attended morning lessons at school, took a nap after lunch in the courtyard, and then headed to Riverhemp for a quick sexual release. (They'd pay a token fee for this at the end of the month, when they got their boarding school allowance). After that, they'd hang out in Aden (where people lived to laugh, and lived on laughter), then return to Dar Saad at night for dinner (also on credit) in a local restaurant. After a sweet wander through the night (Aden's loveliest hours), they'd finally return to the dorms (whose doors hadn't yet closed) to study for a bit.

The day after the students received their monthly allowance, the restaurant owners and Riverhemp prostitutes lined up with their account books (containing all the dates of the students' dinners and dalliances on credit). They came to get what they were owed by their boarding school clientele before the boys spent it elsewhere.

We were endlessly amused by the scene that ensued. Whenever there was a dispute over a meal or fuck that hadn't been paid for, we'd race over to watch the entertaining brawl, and then gossip about it afterwards.

I'd never been to Riverhemp, but the word itself sounded like something out of mythology. For me, someone with a good reputation and a solid religious upbringing, it was enough to make my head spin. (I'd renounced my religious values when I was fourteen, thanks to *The Origins of Marxist Philosophy* by Georges Politzer. Every bookshop in Aden had it in stock. I subsequently entered endless debates and arguments with my father.)

Riverhemp: the word had a certain musicality to it. It was also the name of a tree that grew throughout Aden, and overcame the city's scorching sun and dry climate with death-defying success. It made wonderful shade. All Adenis loved it. They felt connected or akin to it, somehow.

I wanted to visit Riverhemp, just to have a look. And maybe, to follow my best friend from boarding school in his adventures, even if only once.

'At a certain age, the body gains certain natural desires, loud and inevitable. Thirst and flames.' That's what I told Hamid, who took me to Riverhemp and its buzzing atmosphere.

It was as magical as I imagined Venice to be. A few riverhemp trees were scattered around a former oasis that had since turned to desert, interspersed here and there with tents and wooden huts.

This was surrounded by several *locande*, places where people gathered in the afternoon to chew qat. The poor often met there, even if they didn't know each other. They chatted and dreamt and laughed and chewed, high on everything and nothing. Their conversation always came back to sex, in this sandy expanse where in front of them lay:

A porn flick, with the whole oasis as its screen;

A lustful kingdom for the downtrodden classes of society;

An outlet for the lumpenproletariat's desires;

Sexual quarters for the toiling and destitute, to everyone's delight.

The tents were made of two intersecting wooden walls which formed four rooms, screened on the outside with thick canvas. Each tent had four wooden doors, leading to four prostitutes who lounged in the dim light, waiting for customers from the high school, Aden, and all over Yemen.

I would've wanted nothing more than to stay in this bacchanalia forever, were I not swiftly and severely disappointed.

I caught sight of a young man spying though a hole in the fabric. A lame sheikh was doing the same at the tent next door. Berating them was the man known as The Boss – a pimp – someone far from angelic or attractive. His eyes didn't have a modicum of geometric symmetry. Not in shape or position in his skull, or even in how they moved.

Half of the comrades from my party's grassroots organisation were queuing for the tents.

Among them was one of my best friends, who had fled North Yemen for Aden. (In North Yemen, the six goals of the Yemeni revolution were published in the newspaper every day.

After arriving in Aden, my friend wished that 'improving Riverhemp' were the seventh goal. Later, during the depths of heartbreak, we both wished it had been the revolution's only goal!)

The worst part: these prostitutes weren't even attractive. One had gold teeth and a nasty way of smoking cigarettes. Another had teeth so black they instantly extinguished any erotic inclinations.

Leave it to say, dear Wrecker of Pleasures and Earthly Delights: Riverhemp's tents looked nothing like booths of houris on the banks of the river Kawthar in paradise.

My desire withered, and I asked Hamid if we could leave.

My best friend responded with a phrase I won't ever forget.

'Imran, I think you need to see the Doctor.'

I didn't understand. I worried he thought I wasn't up for the adventure, putting it down to fear or impotence.

Fortunately, he noticed my conflicted silence.

'The Doctor doesn't look like them,' he added. 'She's beautiful, and you should see how she moves. She's in her thirties, and she's Ethiopian, with this lovely caramel skin...'

'Yeah?'

'Her skin's the least of it. Anyway, her name's Dina, but she insists on us calling her "Ms. Doctor". She considers her work a service to humanity, but she doesn't fuck on credit. With her, you've gotta pay in advance, and she's not cheap. But she's sweet and gentle, good at talking and getting you ready, professional, and really generous . . . she does what she does out of pure love.'

She considers her work a service to humanity! His words surprised me, and got me pretty horny. I didn't know what to say.

'Ms. Doctor barely ever comes to Riverhemp,' he added. 'And when she does it's just to visit the girls she knows who work here. When she's fucking the Righteous Seekers of Knowledge – students like you and I, who don't dig the commotion around here – she finds someplace else to conduct her training and development. She's got somewhere more secluded, more *aristocratic* than Riverhemp.'

I sighed with relief.

My friend did what needed to be done to help me 'make my mark on history', as he called it: he arranged an appointment for me that Friday, just before everyone went to noon prayer.

A day in time, when light was not made
By the morning sun, but by our own hands

As a Yemeni poet once said.

A day in time, when light was not made by my hands, because I was too nervous. In a dimly lit, abandoned house (in the al-Momadara neighbourhood, on the far side of the outskirts of Sheikh Othman), I was unable to rise to this historic challenge, despite Hamid's support. He had walked with me all the way to her street during Friday prayer, and was waiting for me on the corner.

I was shaking, to be honest, when I knocked on the Doctor's door.

A day in time, when light was not made by the morning sun . . . but by the Doctor's hands, by her scintillating voice, her gentleness, her Abyssinian beauty, and that caramel skin which smelled of jasmine, cloves, and local wildflowers (there was nothing in the world like it). She prepped me like a real doctor, with her pretty face and agile body, her sensual mouth and pure white African teeth. Just kissing her would have been enough for me that day. I'd never been happier.

(How I'd lowered my ambitions! I who had arrived with the enthusiasm of a Kamikazi pilot, the lust of someone who'd escaped from a life in prison.)

She gave me a glass of cold Canada Dry and made conversation. She helped me start talking and loosen up a bit. Then she realised I'd launched myself at her, trying to kiss her, like one of those soppy characters in *Dad over the Tree*, that old Egyptian film. She hesitated a moment, but then readily entered into a game of kisses with me, as if she was my girlfriend, even though the internal regulations of the world's oldest profession state that kisses aren't in a prostitute's playbook.

She noticed the kissing – like a chemical catalyst for horny students intimidated by the forbidden atmosphere – was really easing my nerves. She started touching me gently, with just her fingertips, focusing on the sides of my hips, that was it. She was drawing all my blood towards the area around her magical caresses. She guided me through the rest of the ballet, just her, the way she liked to, sweet, savvy, and endlessly professional.

Then she said those auspicious words, the kind you only hear from intuitive teachers and spiritual guides:

'Aren't you sweet. But you clearly don't know how to *relax*. Don't worry about it. Come back the same time next Friday, for free.'

A torrent of hormones, a wild surge of joy...

Then she popped my cherry. It all happened faster than I'd fantasised, less idyllic than I'd imagined. But I was happy, happier than I could've imagined.

She popped my cherry, dear Snatcher of Souls:

A revolutionary moment, through and through;

The root from which revolutions grew;

My mark on history.

I wanted to race off, leap over the walls of the high school, and cry out to my friends in the dorms, 'Me too, me too!' I wanted to bound into the boarding school courtyard and shout, 'My sword's been used in battle!'

When I said goodbye to Ms. Doctor with a brief kiss, just like they do it in the movies, she spoke these timeless words to me:

'Sweetie, you're a man now, a *real* man.'

I left her house, afraid someone I knew would see me. Shame rippled through me. 'What if my father, Haj Abdullah Abdel Salam, saw me now?' I asked myself.

But there was no one. The streets were bare. Everyone was at Friday prayer, God bless them.

I rushed off to meet Hamid, nearly flying with joy. He was waiting for me at the street corner. (I flew without wings, I walked without touching the ground. Crows and pigeons smiled at me; butterflies loved me, as did the birds.) I hugged him tight, as if we hadn't seen each other in a decade.

I wished I could hug everyone in Aden, everyone I saw leaving the mosque after Friday prayer and rushing off to the qat market.

I was completely thrilled for the whole of that unforgettable day. Thanks to Hamid I'd finally, actually, become a man. A real man!

I felt like I was flying on a magic carpet for the next two days. In people's eyes I saw either blame ('Have you no shame?') or congratulations ('We know! Well done, *mabrouk*!!')

I was still nervous with Ms. Doctor, though. I didn't actually feel victorious until the third or fourth time I went to her by myself. Without Hamid knowing, I went to the old house she rented with her female friends at the edge of al-Momadara.

I became a real man that day, and soon became addicted to my weekly appointment with my beloved Ms. Doctor: always during Friday prayer.

Chapter Three

If I notice the Stealer of Spirits glancing down at his watch, annoyed by how long I've gone on about the doctor (since he's only agreed to listen and respond to my questions as long as they're about Hawiya), I'll say:

'I beg your pardon, dear friend, dear Smiter of Souls, for how long-winded I'm being about Ms. Doctor. But it's only to convince you of how pure my chance relationship with Hawiya was. I know I've got sidetracked, and taken up your precious time – more than necessary, I'm sure. I only really intended to tell you about Suslov's daughter, Hawiya: the abyss! Now, do you mind if I call you "friend"? Because I can only tell my story honestly and fully if I'm speaking to a dear friend.'

My relationship with Hamid deteriorated unexpectedly. He noticed how passionate I'd become about Ms. Doctor. I often saw her without telling him first, and refused to tell him about our encounters or conversations, which he considered to have become dangerously intimate.

Maybe he loved her in one way or another, without realising it. Or maybe he thought that I loved her. Perhaps it was jealousy; who knows. In any case, he became suspicious. Whenever we spoke, he ended up snapping at me.

His suspicions weren't far off. My addiction to the Doctor grew, to the degree that one day I whispered in her ear, 'I love you, Ms. Doctor.'

She laughed gently.

'That's not the way it works, babe!'

'Why not?'

'You're a little student, sweetheart. You haven't even finished high school! And I'm a doctor in her thirties.'

I must have showed how much I resented her response. She ran her fingers through my hair to diffuse my annoyance.

'What do you think I have a doctorate in, Imran darling?' she asked, knowing how much I loved to sing her praises.

'In painting, music, fine arts...'

(I kissed her fingertips. Oh what sweet fingertips!)

Eventually, Hamid and I made up. But our relationship with the Doctor ended painfully and tragically, around the same time.

If the Ender of Earthly Delights asks me why, I'll tell him the calamitous details in full.

At the dawn of Yemen's National Democratic Revolution (at four in the morning, to be precise), State Security forces came and abducted all the Riverhemp prostitutes. All of them at the same time, both inside and outside Riverhemp. They didn't take them to prison, because in the eyes of the revolution, the 'crushed' and downtrodden classes were no more than 'victims of exploitation by their fellow man'. Instead, they took them to Fayoush Tomato Factory in a far-off oasis, forty kilometres from Aden, which canned crushed tomatoes. The prostitutes were to become factory workers there, part of the 'working class'. (Those two words had a sacred, sublime cadence to them in those days).

In other words, they were to join the proletariat, take up the class struggle, and help build the People's Democratic Republic of Yemen. Prostitutes weren't the only ones who required intervention as per revolutionary ideology. Gay men, 'faggots', as the state referred to them, were abducted and taken to Socotra Island for 'reeducation'.

Maybe this campaign was inspired by the Maoist Cultural Revolution, or other revolutionary ideas. Maybe it was an optimistic vision, an innocent plan, or a reckless idiot's decision, but for me and the other high school students, it was a fatal turn of events.

As a result, I held a grudge against the revolution I had loved with all my heart. Even so, I was still committed to it. The way I saw it, 'Comrade Dina' hadn't been 'forced by class oppression to sell her body to gain power', as the revolutionary interpretation that was fashionable at the time would have it. No: Ms. Doctor was a Doctor of Fine Arts, and no one was gentler or lovelier. From the tips of her fingers, poetry and music flowed.

With the skill of a maestro, she conducted the orchestra of my body from one end to the other. She knew how to get your blood flowing, as Hamid put it. She played my skin like a piano, and lovingly brought its dissonant notes into harmony, in a concerto of pleasure. Her fingertips taught me how to read music, how to dance.

She performed her 'service to humanity' with sincerity, love, and dedication.

As my passion for Doctor Dina grew, so did my grudge against the National Democratic Revolution.

I didn't see the Doctor again, and neither did Hamid. Neither one of us was jealous. Our relationship went back to how it had been – almost.

We avoided talking about the Doctor, even if our desire for her nearly killed us, especially during the final months of high school.

I became intensely jealous of Hamid one day. He told me that every time he touched a can of crushed tomatoes made by the hands of proletariats at Fayoush Tomato Factory, he felt a rush of electricity below the waist, a charge coursing through his body.

'Man, I don't know how, but every time I open a can of crushed tomatoes I get so damn hard!'

Our friendship nearly ended with those words.

By the end of high school, I missed Ms. Doctor like I'd never missed anyone before. I needed her so desperately during those grim schooldays.

When I slept on our roof in Aden, dear Reaper, my body's desires were all directed towards the tomato factory, more than forty kilometres away.

But it was Faten's face – sorry, Hawiya's face – that filled the sky. I'd gaze up at it as if in prayer. I stared into it for ages, swam in it, worshipped it. When I imagined her face just before falling asleep, all my tears unseen in the blind man's shop rose up to my eyes.

The Reaper will shake his head with tender sympathy. He'll know what I want to say.

'Forgive me, dear Azazeel, I got distracted again. I got sidetracked from talking about Hawiya, the point of my story. But now you know where I grew up, the political context, and what life was like during the National Democratic Revolution. You might have forgotten everything that happened then. These are basic, trivial details compared to what you see while passing over continents of history and turning points of geography to pluck human souls from their bodies. I know this is just an infinitely small drop in your ocean of space and time, with its endless unfolding vastness, its multiplicities and complexities stretching from the beginning of days until the end of time.'

Chapter Four

P ost on my Facebook wall:

A.E., the official in charge of the Ministry of Education's Scholarship Department in the 1970s in Aden, was beloved by students in my high school class.

He was a typical Adeni through and through: from the way he looked, his sense of humour, the wads of Indian paan masala that were always in his mouth, and his enthusiasm for football matches at al-Hubaishi Stadium in the Crater district. This was particularly true if his favourite team al-Husseini was playing, or its arch-rival al-Ahrar was.

I learned that if you wanted to catch him in a good mood, you had to go to a coffee shop by the stadium, near Sirah fishing port in the Crater district, after a football match al-Husseini had won or al-Ahrar had lost. (When he was at his office in the Ministry, he barely had time for anyone.)

That's what I tried to do one day. (I'd graduated high school and was doing my National Service, teaching maths to eight-

and nine-year-olds in Sheikh Othman Primary School.)
I wanted to know whether my scholarship to study in France
or the German Democratic Republic had been approved.
(I was a candidate in both countries.)

I caught sight of him next to the Graduate School for
Scientific Socialism, that majestic building, just as he was
leaving the stadium. He was with a fellow supporter on their
way to the port, clearly pleased with their team's victory
over their rivals that day.

I was eager to ask him about the fate of my scholarship, and
rushed over to the coffee shop to find him. He tried to calm
me down, and asked if I wanted to join them for a cup of tea,
and in that magical moment when the Sirah sun sets behind the
Shamsan Mountains across the port, his offer was hard to refuse.

'If you had a choice between France and the GDR, *ya ibni*,
which would you pick?' he asked after I sat down.

'France.'

'Why's that?'

'Because I love sunsets.'

'Sorry?'

'I want to see the sunset of capitalism with my own eyes! I'll
have my whole life to help build socialism.'

(Every day we heard in the media – and were thoroughly convinced – that ours was the era of the 'sunset of capitalism,' and the 'dawn of socialism.')

A.E. smiled, and then chuckled a bit. He laughed more, and then more, until he was spluttering he was laughing so hard. (His tongue, I noticed, was tinged with purple from paan masala.)

He didn't explain why he was laughing or what he was thinking.

'Don't you worry about the scholarship,' he finally said, after regaining his composure. Then he added, 'I've got a favour to ask, *ya ibni*.'

'Yes?'

'If you remember this conversation one day, write it down just the way it happened. And don't leave out how hard I laughed at your response – I haven't laughed like that in ages!'

Another side note here, dear Reaper: I can't speak about Suslov's daughter without first speaking for a minute or two about Najaa, a girl I met in Paris.

Arriving in Paris to study wasn't just a turning point for me – it was the big bang itself, and it shook my whole universe.

The beginning of a new life;

And everything in it:

Paris' beauty, days, nights, lights, culture, history, language, museums, people, streets, restaurants, cafés, churches, rivers, beaches, bridges, monuments – it enthralled me, all of it. I felt myself slowly falling in love, becoming part of it.

Homo yemens turned into *Homo sapiens*. I was subsumed into the capital of culture, art, and love, immersed in its language and life. Paris: the one city in the universe with the power to reshape everything about me.

I felt like I fitted in from the moment I arrived, like I'd lived there from the day I was born.

Sometimes when tasting a certain dish for the first time, I had the uncanny feeling it had been my favourite food in a past life. I savoured it with longing: the nostalgia of decades, of eternity.

The strangest thing was that this new love, however intense, didn't detract from my feelings for Aden, or my ever-present memories of its customs, traditions, and every moment of its everyday.

The more I assimilated in Paris, the more my thoughts were filled with Aden. Everything I saw in Paris reminded me of something I'd experienced in Aden, and of the contrast, the chasm between them. The relentless ache of the quotidian.

At every moment, a current flowed between opposite poles: Paris and Aden.

From the minute I began my language studies in Paris, and the first lecture I attended in the university's Faculty of Arts, happiness and good fortune awaited me.

I loved it all fervently: newspapers, magazines, literature (my longstanding passion and sanctuary), and above all, the novel – that hallmark of the modern era (particularly in France). I loved philosophy, anthropology, and every new discovery in science and technology.

But more than anything else, I loved a girl I met in my first lecture at the Faculty of the Arts (most of the students were girls, and easy on the eye). Najaa: her father was Yemeni, her mother was French, and no one was prettier or lovelier.

Integrity, sincerity, and devotion were written into her very DNA.

I raced towards her and she hurtled towards me, from our very first lecture together. Our passion was filled with fateful heartbeats, dreams, and desires.

I was made for Najaa and she was made for me. Our hearts beat to the same rhythm. We both had scholarships, and enough to get by. We studied together, and worked here and there, to earn a bit on the side so we could endlessly travel and discover the world.

Needless to say, Najaa shared my love of revolutions and dreams of a new world. We had the same naïve, enthralling fantasies.

My understanding of revolution changed when I arrived in Paris, and through my relationship with Najaa. After long discussions, endless debates, and even the odd heated argument, she convinced me that the Soviet concept of revolution was not only false, but also hostile to freedom and democracy. (I was a proud Stalinist at heart, even though I denied it vehemently if asked.)

Najaa rewrote my political lexicon, and my heart beat for her in its new revolutionary form. *Left* replaced *proletariat*. *Democracy* took the place of *democratic centralism*. And I abandoned *uprisings* in exchange for *deep social transformations*.

If the Angel of the Dead interrupts at this point and bluntly asks how this happened, I'll admit it wasn't easy. Not for someone who had embraced Marxist-Leninism in Aden after reading a book by French philosopher Georges Politzer. (These were simple, easy-to-understand study materials for French Communist cells in the 1950s, at the height of Stalinism).

Everything Politzer wrote was confirmed when I read about the Second Law of Dialectics at age fourteen. 'Gradual changes lead to a paradigm shift,' it said. Then it offered the phase transition of water from liquid to gas as an example.

The lesson stated something to the effect of: water remains a liquid when at a temperature of 1 degree, 20 degrees, 60 degrees, 90 degrees, 98 degrees, 99 degrees. Then comes the boiling point, the degree signalling the phase transition or paradigm shift: the hundredth degree, queen of degrees, at which point water turns to steam.

The same holds true for the transition from capitalism to socialism: the situation heats up until it reaches a revolutionary boil. At the fabled hundredth degree, capitalism is vaporised and the era of socialism begins!

I was in awe of this hundredth degree: paragon, vanguard, and knight of degrees. Key to a revolutionary future, door to paradise. I became enamoured with it, longed for it. To me, it was like a fantastical beast or the hundredth name of God!

Najaa managed to dispel my Marxist-Leninist convictions when she told me one day, with that typical cleverness and good humour of hers, 'If I were water, I'd hate turning into gas over the hob. I hate fire. I'd much rather evaporate under the sun . . . Out in the open air, like seawater.'

I tipped my hat to her! And renounced Stalinism forevermore. My relationship with revolution became like my relationship with the sea.

Our yearly pilgrimage became le Fête de l'Humanité, the annual festival of the French Communist Party newspaper, and a longstanding French tradition. Over three days in the first half of September, people from all parts of French society – and all over the world – converge on the outskirts of Paris. At night we slept there in a tent, and during the day we visited booths of all the countries in the world. We talked with everyone, danced and sang revolutionary songs with the bands (traditional ones and contemporary ones too). The atmosphere of humanitarianism was intoxicating.

The crowds all came together in the festival's main open space on Sunday afternoon, in a massive ceremony of music and speeches.

We raised our hands to sing the l'Internationale with hundreds of thousands of other people, our voices united. Sometimes, in the middle of this human roar, a few tears slipped out despite our efforts to hold them back.

High on the festival, we could forget that we lived in an age where dollars fly around everywhere. Where the forces of finance, banks, and stock exchanges pull the strings, more so than ever before in history. Where the market economy bears down on all humankind. (Everyone kneels in praise of it, everyone, without exception.)

Its selfishness throttles humanity, and threatens to wipe out the future of our planet earth.

But in our dancing and celebration we forgot these bitter truths. Instead we awaited the sunset of capitalism, exploitation, and dictatorial regimes, and the dawn of a new world, a world of justice, socialism, and light.

The world of higher beings and Nietzsche's last man, in the 'Blue Planet Archipelago', as Najaa and I liked to call the earth, the realm of the future.

Najaa was a dreamer just like me, innocent and sincere. She was the love of my life; I'll never love anyone as truly as I loved her. A queen among queens of the universe. A beauty queen par excellence. My only god.

I loved her, as you know, dear Reaper. That glow will never fade.

We had practically everything in common, from our studies in literature (an innate passion), to our love for restaurants and trying new foods. I watched Najaa's slow grace, tenderness, and affection as she devoured seafood, savoured champagne, and discoursed on all kinds of topics, over a soundtrack she had chosen to complement that exact moment and place. I understood how deep her relationship was with life, art, and beauty.

Let's go back, now, to the two of us celebrating her twentieth birthday on a terrace restaurant in Corsica on 12 March 1981. She sat in front of me, and behind her was the glistening sea. Ships bound for Sardinia and the south of France lay to the west, hundreds of sailboats to the east. Pure blue in front of us, mountains in the distance. Flocks of seagulls tirelessly wheeled, dove, and squawked. One landed on a wooden fence behind Najaa (a slight dizziness overtook me whenever I looked at her, a delicious dizziness). Springtime sun. I closed my eyes to drink in its radiance. It enveloped Najaa as she animatedly discussed one subject after the next. (For me, there was nothing more captivating than her voice.)

I imagined her ten years from then (she'd be Department Chair at the University, I'd be a researcher at the national research centre). We'd be celebrating her thirtieth birthday on a hotel restaurant terrace, next to Salah El Deen's citadel in Taba, Sinai (our eternal refuge, our personal Venice). The desert of prophets and poets extending all around us. Distant dusty mountains, the same colour as those near Aden, whose peaks we'd often hiked, just the two of us. Behind Najaa the Gulf of Aqaba. A mythical blue. Waters so transparent that reefs deep below the surface can be seen clearly by the naked eye. A sacred desert sunset. To the south, Mount Sinai (we hiked to the summit to see the sunset and slept there several times), Moses, the holy flame. The point where the seven heavens kiss the earth, with nothing in between.

The link between our past and present selves: the sea. We were both crazy about swimming in warm waters. Najaa was the most beautiful fish in the sea; like me, she seemed at home among the waves. We could only truly breathe when we were in the water, and when we were too far from the sea, it felt like we were gasping for air. On Aden's beaches we were often alone. We spent the most beautiful and intimate days of our lives on Imran Island.

Najaa and I were passionate about culture, too. Undeniably fond of films, the cinema, virtual reality, and computer animation (the science of appearances, as Najaa called it). But more than anything we loved reading, writing, the smell of paper and ink, visual arts, music, theatre. 'Sciences of the subconscious, the only thing you can really get to the bottom of,' as she also used to say.

Najaa and I traversed more than a third of the world before having children . . . I'll add here the phrase that Najaa dreamed we would say, three decades after we joined our lives: 'We wandered the second third with our children, and we'll wander the last third, the rest of our lives, just us two again.'

(Najaa was from a family where people lived a long time, fathers like grandfathers before them.)

I'm sorry to say (even though the word 'sorry' seems so trite, so infinitely feeble) that our plan never came to fruition. You know this better than anyone, dear Destroyer of Dreams.

The reason: Saint-Michel metro station in the heart of the Latin Quarter in Paris. (I can't go there anymore.)

The date: 25 July 1995. (I can hardly bear mentioning it.) It was the height of the dark Algerian years, when Paris trembled in fear of Salafi terrorist bombings.

You were there, dear Azazeel, harvesting souls from their scattered remains, charred skulls, and what was left of their belongings. Cluster bombs planted in a rubbish bin had exploded in a narrow corridor packed with Metro passengers.

(Our language's agricultural metaphors here are like salt in the wound.)

Najaa was in the Metro station, on her way back from the Rue des Écoles in the Latin Quarter. She was carrying a fountain pen, a handful of pencils (she knew how much I loved writing in pencil), and a few books she'd bought from Gibert-Joseph Bookstore near the Saint-Michel metro in the Latin Quarter.

And in her belly: our first child, in its fifth month, a girl. We wanted to name her Scheherazade, or Helen.

An inconsequential detail: I was waiting for her at home, cooking us dinner. I'd prepared a Yemeni dish called *alzerbian* (an Adeni version of biryani), and was listening to lively Yemeni music on the record player, trusting that the possibility of terrorist explosions was infinitely small. Those things only happen to other people.

In the blink of an eye, my life careened from absolute bliss into utter hell.

Part of my mind stopped working that day, forever.

Part of my life stopped that day, forever.

Let me stop here too, dear Reaper. For a few minutes.

In my chest, as you know, is a boundless, crushing pain, endlessly bleeding. And hatred – as powerful as a volcano, as vast as an ocean of darkness.

Chapter Five

Post on my Facebook wall:

In the early 1970s, the People's Democratic Republic of Yemen was ruled by young people who lacked experience or qualifications. Despite this, they had absolute confidence that theirs was the best of all the Arab regimes. They were open to the world and the future, and marched towards 'the hallmark of the age,' as they called it. They hoped that the National Democratic Revolution would provide a shortcut, so they could cross from feudalism to socialism (without having to pass through capitalism on the way).

The era of socialism would begin in just fifteen or twenty-five years (according to ideologues who had a great love for forward-looking theoretical debate, and for seeking out signs of Marxist-Leninism when divining the future in coffee grounds.) Society would be free of man's exploitation of his fellow man (thanks of course to the support of our Soviet comrades).

'The hallmark of the age was the victory of socialism, and the defeat of capitalism'- as God Almighty had decreed.

Since I'd first arrived in Paris, and during every summer vacation that Najaa and I travelled to Aden, I always wondered what had happened to Hawiya.

Ancient Uncle Saif had passed away, and his oldest son Alwan, who could see quite well, had taken his place. His shop was no longer a haven for lovers to meet (without either of them uttering a word of farewell before one of them went abroad to study).

In any case, Hawiya's mother Fairuz no longer came to our run-down street in Sheikh Othman, the stage our shared childhood had played out on.

There was little chance of approaching their new luxury villa in the distant upscale neighbourhood of Khormaksar, either. Suslov was a rising political and party leader (with a political position in the ruling party). There was much talk about his Kissenger-esque diplomatic skills (or Gromyko-esque, as should be said, for Andrei Gromyko, Soviet Minister of Foreign Affairs at the time). Many said he could be a contender for the next Minister of Foreign Affairs, and that he would certainly take political office after the next Party Conference.

The only things I knew about Suslov's family were related to the meetings and activities of senior politicians and party officials: their families, daily lives, struggles, and official trips. And that their only child, Hawiya, was tossed about in this whirlpool. Plus, that they were about to move to an even more aristocratic villa on the edge of a cliff overlooking the sea, in the Tawahi neighbourhood, even further away.

Adeni life, dear Reaper, was secular and modern in those days. Women didn't wear religious clothes. They were educated, worked, and took part in senior party leadership. There were co-ed schools. Books (especially progressive and revolutionary ones) were everywhere. Family Law granted women important, tangible rights, and governed social life.

Students could easily travel to other socialist countries to study. Priority was given to children of the 'toiling' classes. In other words: those from certain class origins. This was marked on their nomination forms, although the income threshold was quite low.

The bourgeoisie dug himself a fine well
When the poor man stumbled, in he fell

As a popular poet said at the time.

Modernity emerged before our very eyes. People always find new things alluring.

The national beer brewery, for example: Sirah Brewery, named after the famous citadel in the port of Sirah in the Crater district. As a mark of modernity, one could openly drink alcohol in bars in Aden.

Amusingly, some people asked the bar staff not to remove the empty bottles from their table before they were done for the night. As the number of empties grew, and became more and more visible, so did the drunkard's faith he was part of modernity and progressive thought!

(Meanwhile, a famous military tribesman was smuggling alcohol through Bab al-Mandab, and was on his way to becoming president of North Yemen.)

The strangest thing was that people didn't differentiate between one presumptive trait of modernity and another.

Believe it or not, dear Smiter of Souls, certain highly respectable families believed that modernity meant watching porn together after lunch or dinner: young and old, family and guests, 'just like people in developed countries do'. (That's what they believed!)

The worst part: sometimes it was S&M.

'How inappropriate,' mumbles the Wrecker of Pleasures and Ender of Delights as he scratches his head. He's troubled by these dark disclosures about humankind's stupidity. A shadow of sorrow crosses his brow. He takes a deep breath.

He shakes his head again, and I continue.

Dearest Azazeel: when it came to this aspect of modernity in particular, Suslov embodied the dialectical relationship between theory and practice.

He was around the same age as my schoolteachers, so about ten years older than me. He grew up in the Awaliq Mountains, and when he moved to Aden, he lived with some distant relatives who resided on the outskirts and worked in the city. He was destitute when he arrived. His mother had died when he was young, and his father depended on him to send money for the family.

He had to work as a servant while finishing his studies. He was full of energy, tactful, and successful. The revolution against English colonialism gave him an opportunity to rise quickly in politics. He became a prominent young fighter just before independence in 1967, a 'daring guerilla' as people said.

His situation changed when the Left arrived in power (after the coup against the opportunistic Right on 22 June 1969).

I still remember, dear Stealer of Spirits, when he used to come to our street. (He'd started flirting with Fairuz, a girl from the neighbourhood, at around age seventeen.)

Sometimes he and I chatted on the corner, while he waited for Fairuz to come out onto her balcony so he could smile at her, or wink, or send her a message.

He was serious but kind, skilled in all types of conversation: from humour (he was an encyclopaedia of jokes) to political theory. He excelled in the latter. After he returned from studying Marxist-Leninist science in Moscow, he became the party's official Marxist-Leninist ideologue.

When we were young, we listened to him with wide-eyed admiration as he stood on the street corner and spoke about his real interests: sex and 'lacy infrastructure' (suspenders).

Perhaps with his Don Juan demeanour, tales of romantic exploits, and extensive experience, he was trying to overcome his sense of inferiority for having worked as a servant in Aden. Or maybe he really was obsessed with suspenders.

Riverhemp City: he knew it by heart. I remember when he explained female anatomy and his theory on vaginas.

'If you wanna know what a woman's vagina looks like, just look at her mouth. It's the same shape, colour, and size,' he always said. His other vague, odd theories also aroused my interest at that age.

Our street abounded with theories, especially those about vaginas. All the different variations aroused my interest.

I remember, for example, our rabble-rousing neighbour and her alcoholic husband, whose arguments could be heard up and down the street every night. (She had a booming voice that shook the walls.)

At the climax of their thunderous row, she let loose a strange popular idiom that's stuck in my mind ever since: 'Nothing lasts in this life except veins in the vagina!'

So whenever I heard Suslov giving a speech on the radio or television (after he became the party's official ideologue and never tired of discussing the 'hallmarks of the age') I was reminded of my childhood, and all the theories on vaginal anatomy and morphology I heard on the street corner.

I asked after any news of Suslov's family every summer that Najaa and I visited Aden from Paris, dear Reaper. That raised some eyebrows.

In the early eighties, I learned that Suslov's adventures with his secretaries and an array of other girls were the subject of much gossip, and that his relations with his wife were no longer civil, but tantamount to civil war.

Then in the mid-eighties, I found out that his wife had taken revenge. She'd begun a relationship with his arch-rival (a highly important political leader): a man more senior in rank, and more devilish. As a result, their small family fractured.

Matters were made worse when the South Yemen Civil War broke out in January 1986, between rival factions of the ruling Yemeni Socialist Party. (A staggering 13,000 people were killed.)

The Civil War split the ruling party and army along regional tribal lines. It revealed that ideals of socialism, internationalism, and the proletariat were just masks worn by illiterate Marxists. In reality, they were no more than barbaric, backwards tribes.

In the lead-up to the 1986 Civil War, Suslov and Fairuz's conflict grew fiercer and bloodier. They launched the mother of all battles and aired each other's dirty laundry with malice and a heinous spirit of revenge.

And their only daughter endured it all: Hawiya, poor thing, neglected by her parents in their relentless daily struggle. She was left only with the dream of fleeing far from that hell.

Chapter Six

Post on my Facebook wall:

I don't intend to tell the Angel of Revolutions about the fourth deposit in my bank statement of personal activities during the Yemeni Revolution, from when I was a student in Aden. It's more trivial than the previous three.

I'll post it here instead, for the Angels of Facebook Revolutions:

In the early seventies, I was a delegate to the Democratic Youth Federation of Yemen's first party conference for the Sheikh Othman and Surrounding Neighbourhoods Branch. The conference aimed to unite three separate sections of youth across the nation. (These later formed one ruling party: the Yemeni Socialist Party, 'whose voice rose above the rest.')

The conference passed fairly uneventfully, albeit the last time it did so.

It was held in the same desert school where we later organised literacy classes. Discussions lasted all day.

By evening, three people (including me) from the three youth divisions were tasked with drafting resolutions to be discussed the next day.

We agreed on nearly everything, except for superficial grammatical details (just two or three lines) in our draft statement, entitled 'Support for the Revolution in Mozambique, from the Youth of Sheikh Othman and Surrounding Neighbourhoods.' We knew how crucial our resolution was. It could shift the balance of power across the whole earth, and on neighbouring planets too.

(The three of us had heard there was a revolution, but we didn't know anything about it. We didn't even know where Mozambique was, except for that it was in Africa. Despite this, we became official spokespersons for the Youth of Sheikh Othman regarding support for the Mozambique Revolution. (Most of them hadn't even heard of Africa, but that's another story.))

We debated until four in the morning, but couldn't reach an agreement.

Finally, I went home. My parents were so anxious that they hadn't slept at all: my mother had cried gallons of tears, and my father had repeated his nightly *witr* prayers a thousand times. They were terrified I'd been swept away by some political disaster, the kind that poured down in torrents during those years.

The conference proceedings were delayed the next morning because we hadn't been able to agree. Finally, just before noon, the senior leaders intervened and resolved our dispute over Mozambique.

Perhaps it was thanks to the 'revolutionary aspirations and education' I displayed at this conference (the featherweight division) that I was nominated to attend a larger one (the heavyweight division): the National Liberation Front (NLF)'s Fifth General Conference for Political Organising. The NLF was the main force in power at the time. (After the British left, it would seize power from its rival, the Front for the Liberation of Occupied South Yemen (FLOSY). Shortly after that, the NLF became the Yemeni Socialist Party, 'whose voice rose above the rest.')

First, I had to fill out an application form.

Just like all other forms I filled out in the People's Democratic Republic of Yemen, there were two more boxes after the spaces to write your name, and place and date of birth. Two boxes of critical importance:

1) Class identity
2) Class origins

The first was relatively easy: Student (petite bourgeoisie).

That's what I wrote, because students formed part of the petite bourgeoisie, according to laws of physics and language in vogue at the time.

Revolution-approved class identities included poor farmer, and (if you were really lucky) working class. Lords and the bourgeoisie had fallen out of fashion, and were now nowhere to be found. The first had been disposed of by glorious peasant uprisings, and the second fled when their property was nationalised.

I didn't know what to put under 'class origins'. My father, Haj Abdullah Abdel Salam, owned a small restaurant on the outskirts of the outskirts of Sheikh Othman. It specialised in Hadrami fish dishes.

Luckily, I didn't have bourgeoise roots, and wasn't obliged to write the worst possible response in this critical box: bourgeoisie. (That would've been the end of me.) But unfortunately, I couldn't write either of two relatively good responses: revolutionary intellectual, or poor farmer. My father was neither.

Two possibilities remained. The preferable option, which would open doors for me: working class. And a worse option, which would arouse mistrust and herald disaster: petite bourgeoisie. Party literature aimed all its suspicious and insults at the petite bourgeoisie, those 'revolutionary hypocrites'.

I didn't know what to write. I left the space blank. I feared the consequences of the second answer, and was unsure I deserved the honour and nobility of the first.

Criticism rained down on me during the preparatory meeting to elect delegates for the Fifth General Conference. Apparently, leaving this box blank indicated 'weak sensibilities and beliefs, and poor revolutionary consciousness'. Unbelievable!

The problem was that when they wanted to fill it in for me, they couldn't agree on a response either.

A heated debate ensued at this historic preparatory meeting about my class origins, and the entire political elite of the People's Democratic Republic of Yemen had something to contribute. Half of them favoured the first answer, and the other half favoured the second.

Believe it or not, dear Angel of Facebook Revolutions:

After a long debate, Comrade Salmeen (as Salim Ruabi Ali was known), the President of the People's Democratic Republic of Yemen himself, had an idea:

'Let's form a committee to go to comrade Imran's father's restaurant, and count the number of spoons.' (Local Yemeni restaurants never had knives or forks.)

My class origins would be determined by whether or not the spoons exceeded a certain watershed number (to be determined by the committee in a closed meeting). Then the committee would fill out the form accordingly.

A committee was formed, and they headed to my father's restaurant. Then they held a closed-door meeting to determine what number represented the tipping point between petite bourgeoisie spoons and working class spoons.

In other words: the number of damn spoons is what turns a working class man into the petite bourgeoisie.

In other words: it was the hundredth degree from Politzer's book, but in reverse. (Once again, gradual change led to a paradigm shift, but here the next stage was worse.)

After an extensive discussion about this intractable theoretical conundrum of utmost importance, my class origins were determined:

Petite bourgeoisie!

Curse of curses: the class of 'original sin and inherent hypocrisy!'

So I didn't go to the conference. Attending the Democratic Youth Federation of Yemen's party conference for Youth of Sheikh Othman and Surrounding Neighbourhoods was my greatest historical contribution to Yemen's National Democratic Revolution. That was it.

In the late seventies, I returned to Aden on my first summer holiday from Paris.

'How did the second youth conference go?' I eagerly asked a young man from our street who had attended the conference. 'Have you drafted the resolution on supporting the Revolution in Mozambique?'

'Man, it's almost the eighties,' he told me, rather harshly I thought. 'The revolution's not still taking baby steps like it was back when you were at the conference. The revolution's grown up.'

'What do you mean? What's happened?'

'We model things after our Soviet comrades now. By the time we arrive at the conferences, all the resolutions, recommendations, and other party literature is already drafted. It comes straight from the senior leadership, and all we need to do is vote on it. There's no need to discuss it, not like the early days when you were around.'

Post on my Facebook wall:

Four years after the South Yemen Civil War in 1986, North Yemen and South Yemen were unified, on 22 May 1990. Then, just four years after that, the Yemeni Civil War broke out. A coalition of Salafi, tribal, military, and jihadi forces in power invaded the South in a war that lasted for two months. It ended on an ominous day: 7 July 1994.

As a result of the war, the South was thoroughly looted. Its political, military, and civilian elite were exiled, co-ed schooling immediately ceased, and all traces of civil society were erased. The hijab and niqab became commonplace, and Aden's secular identity was effectively stamped out.

Sirah Beer factory and all the city's bars closed. This wasn't just to help line the pockets of senior officials and military men who sold contraband liquor, but was for the simple reason that anyone caught drinking alcohol would be whipped in the street.

The war had been building for a year or two. A hundred and ninety leaders of the Yemeni Socialist Party and the Left, as well as prominent civilian figures, had been assassinated. Al-Qaeda proudly claimed responsibility. The regime's 'hidden fingers' had of course cooperated, with the Salafis, and Muslim Brotherhood's approval and support.

When Najaa and I visited Aden that first summer after the 1986 War, it felt like the People's Democratic Republic of Yemen had fallen into a bottomless abyss. I recited the Fatiha over it; may it rest in peace.

Two days after we arrived, the answer to my question about Suslov's family was like a slap in the face:

'Faten fled to the North.'

The Marxist-Leninist School's headmaster's daughter fled progressive Yemen to regressive Yemen?

It was a shock I wouldn't forget, dear Snatcher of Souls.

'Fled to the North' was a vague but awful phrase often heard throughout the seventies and eighties, when the borders between the two countries were closed, and security control was strict. A well known euphemism, it implied that the person who 'fled to the North' had been abducted and killed.

It meant, quite simply: assassinated.

And since Yemen is a country that respects principles of geometric symmetry, the phrase had a cousin in the North: 'fled to the South'. In other words: secretly assassinated there, without a trace of who the victim was or how they died.

Where was she really? Should I read the Fatiha over her? Could she really be dead, like everyone else who 'fled to the North'? Impossible. Her father was a senior military leader, who had become increasingly important since the deadly 1986 War. People who 'fled to the North' were always political opponents, religious reactionaries, or critics of the regime. Or, they fell within the umbrella accusation invoked by state media a thousand times a day: the counter-revolution. (This was before it was replaced by other terms: the 'opportunist right' and 'opportunist left'. Oh, capricious ideology.)

Where was she really? A horrible mystery, the greatest puzzle of them all.

Aden was nearly unrecognisable when Najaa and I arrived for a holiday in the winter of 1995. (We celebrated her thirty-forth birthday on Imran Island. We had the beach to ourselves, and it was the most beautiful day ever. I'll never forget the date: 12 March 1995.)

After the 1994 Yemeni Civil War, Aden became a city humiliated, the spoils of war. The tribes and obscurantists viciously plundered its land and riches.

At one point as we were driving, I saw a man cross the street. He was alone, and seemed intent on not being recognised. He'd lost all the glory for which I'd once known him.

We stopped the car, and Najaa and I went over to him.

I introduced myself so he'd remember me. I realised that otherwise he wouldn't have recognised me or remembered sitting on the street corner together when we were kids.

His eyes had lost their gleam. His gaze was dim, hazy, lost in space. It held only anxiety, and fear of something.

I introduced my wife, who naturally reached out her hand to shake his. He excused himself from shaking her hand, saying he'd just washed for prayer.

A surge of electricity coursed through me, dear Reaper. A slight, an insult. Blasphemy! An inconceivable about-face: from the loftiest atheism of Marxist-Leninism to the basest superficiality, pretence, and blatant theatrics, with no sense of common courtesy. The headmaster of Aden's Graduate School for Marxist-Leninist Science refused to shake my wife's hand, because he had just washed for prayer and didn't want to negate his ritual ablution.

I pitied him, and Lenin too!

('Me too,' interjects the dear old Reaper, without realising he's even said anything.)

Lenin – may he rest in peace – moans twice in his mausoleum in Red Square. Once, at hearing this. And once more, because today his mausoleum in Red Square sits before Kenzo and Chanel and other beacons of capitalism's triumph in Russia.

Suslov didn't want to speak with us for long. He was pale and thin, a shadow of his old self. He looked like other people I'd seen muttering meaningless words to themselves, or ceaselessly murmuring recitations of religious prayers and verses from the Quran.

I wanted to ask about his daughter, Hawiya. No. It was hard to bring up such a sensitive subject when he seemed so nervous and unwilling to talk, and wouldn't even shake hands because – as he said with a dark and listless smile – he'd, just washed for prayer.

I said goodbye, in disbelief: Suslov, the headmaster of the School for Marxist-Leninist Science, refused to shake my wife's hand because he had just washed for prayer.

I tense up whenever I remember this, dear Reaper, and a dense dizziness sweeps over me.

(I hear the Snatcher of Souls interrupting me again: 'Me too.')

Chapter Seven

My friend M. H. posted this on her Facebook wall:

The Last Soldier to Uphold the Law in South Yemen

After the war of '94, when Aden was invaded by tribes from North Yemen, a decree was issued banning cars without number plates from going through checkpoints.

One day, a senior tribal sheikh from the North and his entourage were coming from Sana'a, and arrived at the second checkpoint into Aden. Ten cars, all without number plates. They wanted to go through the checkpoint.

The Southern soldier stationed there stopped them.

Sheikh: I'm Sheikh H!

Soldier: None of your cars have number plates, and I've got orders.

Sheikh: I told you, I'm Sheikh H!

Soldier: I've never heard of you, and I don't care.

H ordered his entourage to go ahead and cross the checkpoint. They all started driving. The soldier got angry, raised his gun, and fired a single shot in the air.

Then he saw all the cars turn around and start heading back towards him.

He bolted to the nearest security station, shouting 'H and his men are after me!'

Everyone in the station hightailed it out of there.

H arrived screaming, 'Where's the solider that shot at us?'

When no one responded, he told his men to fire a bazooka at the building, and they did. The rocket exploded on the second floor, and incinerated all the civil records of everyone in Sheikh Othman in Aden.

The President was furious when he heard the news, and convened an urgent meeting.

The result: an urgent order was issued – 'the solider must apologise to Sheikh H!'

He was the last Southern soldier to try to uphold the law after the 1994 Yemeni Civil War, as people of the South were accustomed to doing.

For the South, this infamous incident was the beginning of the end. Soon after, the Northern tribes looted all that was left.

My friend K. H. posted this on his Facebook wall:

I've told you again and again:

This city is a whore in a niqab, working the streets while feigning virtue.

This city is an infidel claiming he believes. For every minaret that's erected, a new prostitution ring springs up.

There's nothing worse than a city where half the people are informants and the rest are pimps.

Take it as a rule: a city filled with minarets is one where whores are doing it in dark alleyways leading to the mosque.

That kind of city is far from pure; leave it before you're cursed.

I'm still surprised when people ask, 'Why do you hate Sana'a?'

I don't just hate it. I despise it. I despise it.

A year after Najaa died, in the summer of 1996, I arrived in Sana'a: the capital of unified Yemen. I was in my forties, and it was the first time I'd ever been there. The moment I discovered my new capital was one I won't ever forget. Sana'a is a city of uniquely beautiful architecture, amazing weather, and incredible backwardness and hypocrisy.

Sana'a almost seemed to float above the earth, fluttering majestically from a lofty height of nearly two kilometres. (The same elevation as the 'Eagle's Nest', Alamut Castle, which was once the base of the Hashishin, a secret medieval Ismaili order, before it was seized by Hassan-i Sabbah in 1090.)

Sana'a: an Alamut Castle as big as a city!

There was no better place in the world to forget Najaa: nothing there reminded me of her. In Sana'a, I sometimes managed to forget the eternal knife in my back, the wound that continued to ache and bleed.

I loved Sana'a for that alone, both tenderly and savagely.

I stayed in a hotel on Hadda Street for a few days when I first arrived. It wasn't far from the flat where my sister Samia lived with her husband and children. She was a doctor, and had moved from Aden to Sana'a for work.

I'd practically raised Samia myself: I helped her in school, and with revolutionary youth and student activities. I even instructed her in cultural groups that trained top youth to join the Yemeni Socialist Party, 'the party of the working class and all other toiling forces,' as it was eloquently called back then.

She soon became more active than I was, and more revolutionary. Even as a young student, she was considered an eminent Marxist-Leninist party member.

When I arrived at her flat in the summer of 1996, she was another woman. She performed all the prayers, even optional *duha* and *witr* ones, and countless extra Sunnah practices too. Every wall and door of every room of her house was covered with prayers in her handwriting. A prayer for embarking on travel, a prayer for return from travel, a prayer for knocking on a door, a prayer for entering through a door, a prayer for exiting through a door, a prayer for the kitchen, a prayer for putting on shoes, a prayer for taking off shoes, a prayer for almonds and pistachios, a prayer for Vimto, a prayer for going to bed, a prayer to dispel nightmares, a prayer for nightmares . . .

I felt like I'd landed on another planet. You would've been just as shocked too, dear Azazeel, if your little sister, a respected doctor – who wore a miniskirt in high school, and was once a prominent feminist revolutionary activist – now wore a heavy, black Talibanesque niqab. You'd wish the explanation was that 'the mother of all jinns had swallowed you whole,' as the old saying goes.

When men headed to qat gatherings on Sana'a's calm afternoons, all kinds of imaginable and unimaginable things happened in the city. There were amicable qat gatherings (where friendships lifted a little weight off people's overburdened lives), and Mafia-like qat gatherings (where tribal feuds mixed with political intrigue). There were tales of amazing sex, and private cars taking people to drinking binges and mass orgies behind closed doors. There were whores so nasty they'd turn a jinn's hair white, and religious hypocrisy so shameless it laughed in the face of the devil himself.

A million cities are hidden within Sana'a. A million secrets and dreams are hidden in the minds of every woman there. A million sorrows and pains, a million heartaches and little joys.

Sana'a is a city where suppressed memories and secrets abound. They dance through the streets, first in a classical waltz, and then in a traditional tribal *bara'a,* daggers bared.

Sana'a is a city where sparkling streams meet fetid swamps.

Sana'a is face-off between a soft-spoken caterpillar and a hedgehog bristling above it. The caterpillar is cocooned in a thousand hijabs and niqabs, and the hedgehog has *janabi* daggers and swords for spikes.

Sana'a is a beautiful young child, raped by a tribal sheikh who hasn't washed the stench of qat from his mouth in seventy years.

A minnow crushed by massive tribal octopi (as they crush everyone under their sway). Each octopus has a thousand tentacles, each tentacle a thousand suckers.

Sana'a is a jewel in the hand of a pirate. Dark snot on a rose.

I love this city, despite myself. I love it more and more.

And forgive me for whispering, as I tremble with shame: deep down, I desperately desire it.

I dropped by my sister's flat on one of those sweet early Sana'a days, and found her with a friend in a niqab who looked like someone straight out of Adel Imam's film *Birds of Darkness.*

The strange thing was that they didn't shut the door to the room they were in when they saw me come into the flat, as women usually do around a man who isn't family. Instead, my sister introduced me to her friend, who took the initiative and extended her hand to shake mine (quite unusual for Salafi women).

I remembered Suslov, who refused to give my wife a handshake, even though shaking her hand was an honour he didn't deserve.

This woman wore gloves to protect her skin from touching mine, of course. She wore a long, billowing black abaya and a niqab that revealed nothing but her eyes – her eyes, which told me that I knew them;

I didn't know them;

I knew them vaguely;

I didn't know them at all.

She was the pinnacle of grace. Her hijab flowed over a dangerously alluring body. There was a surprising contradiction between this stranger's conservative Salafi air, and her hijab that so cleverly clung to her curves.

Even though I could only see her eyes, I could've sworn it was Hawiya, had my sister not said (to my instant disappointment), 'This is Ama al-Rahman, a friend of mine and a wonderful preacher . . . and this is my brother, a literature scholar who lives in Paris.'

'Nice to see you guys,' I responded.

To see you! These words slipped out unconsciously, dear Stealer of Spirits. The only part of this girl I saw was her deadly eyes.

Then her voice (just as fatal) and pure Sana'a accent crushed any hope that this was Hawiya. (Hawiya definitely had an Adeni accent. I was sure of it, even though I'd never heard her speak, despite the many hours we'd spent in silent exchange, playing our game of statues in the blind man's shop.)

'God bless your evening. Your presence brightens our city.'

She uttered the formulaic greeting in a strangely sultry voice.

A ruinous voice.

With an accent from the mountains of Sana'a, light years away from an Adeni one.

'Do you want to have some tea with us? Or coffee, Vimto, or Coca Cola?' my sister asked.

'No, thanks. I was just looking for the notebook I left here yesterday; it has all my childhood friends' phone numbers. They're coming to visit, and I need to get back to the hotel.'

I left, haunted by Ama al-Rahman's sexy gaze that contradicted her conservative appearance (she was a carnival of contradictions, to be honest). Her eyes seemed familiar somehow. They unearthed strange, sorrowful feelings deep in my unconscious. They shone when she looked at me. It was like a code I didn't know how to crack.

I left my sister's flat with a clear idea of what sort of person this Sana'a fanatic who had influenced my sister was. My sister – now obsessed with prayers, even extra Sunnah ones – was the same woman once obsessed with didactic and historical materialism, back when I was a young 'fanatic' myself. She'd exchanged one religion for another.

I'd thought proselytisers only succeeded with the poor and illiterate.

But I was mistaken: they even succeeded with daughters from far-flung, mountainous, tribal parts of Sana'a. And with my city-born sister, who was armed with a top degree in medicine, and Marxist-Leninist studies too.

Resentment on top of resentment: my secular teachings had failed my little sister. I'd been defeated by an obscurantist proselytiser from Sana'a, someone who praised and plotted terrorist explosions like the one that turned all of my dreams to nightmares.

My secret loathing swelled.

Three days later, I was in my room at the hotel. I heard a thundering roar that sounded like a demonstration. I opened the window, and saw a flood of black engulfing the street. A women's demonstration. A thousand bodies concealed in black hijabs and niqabs, crowded together in rows, each woman accompanied by a young child: a boy or girl. (According to Salafi beliefs, 'a woman of faith shouldn't go out into the street by herself.' She needs a *mahram* – unmarriageable kin – if she's going somewhere where there will be men. Or if she's around other women in public, she needs to be accompanied by a young child.)

The wave of women advanced, carrying signs with slogans I couldn't make sense of: *Sharia permits four wives* (next to a picture of a hand with the thumb curled towards the palm, waving four fingers, from the index finger to the pinky).

Another slogan: *Parliament's draft law prohibiting girls under the age of eighteen from marriage conflicts with the sharia's teachings.*

And another: *The draft law forbidding violence against women discriminates against the principles of the sharia.*

And another: *The draft law prohibiting men from beating women violates men's rights, as set forth in the Surah of Women, verse 34.*

What was this Quranic verse? 'And those women you fear may rebel: admonish, and abandon them in their beds, and smack them.'

I looked down at the torrent of black flooding the street, and asked myself whether this was a nightmare or reality. The scene was more frightening than a horror film. As a modern man, I had a severe allergy to obscurantists and terrorists. I felt a violent urge to vomit.

I need your help, dear Reaper, really I do:

Is there a hidden moral in this succession of marches: from those chanting 'Who the fuck threw that!' behind Hassani when we were kids, to 'Violence for violence' during the Seven Glorious Days, to 'Sharia permits four?'

Are we destined to be no more than the universe's guinea pigs? Does life have meaning, a goal? Purpose or significance? Or are our lives ruled by a changeable, metaphysical clock, whose hands sweep past in an instant?

Is life just a play written by lunatics, performed in a mental asylum?

Where am I now? Where have I been living, where do I live now? What awaits us in decades to come? In centuries to come?

I stood in front of the window, staring at this surreal, repugnant scene in disbelief. The telephone in my room rang. A young man from reception told me that someone in the lobby wanted to see me.

I went downstairs and found, to my surprise, the spry, dynamic woman who'd been at the front of the march (the main organiser, as I later found out). She'd entered the hotel as the march crossed the street, without anyone noticing, in a society where a woman entering a hotel by herself raises eyebrows.

She was sitting on a couch in the lobby waiting for me. I walked up to her, confused.

Her religious greeting: 'May the peace, mercy, and blessings of God be upon you.'

My response: 'Hey, how's it going?'

Her response: 'Thanks be to God.'

Then she began talking to me excitedly, as if I supported her party and religious ideals. She proudly told me how huge the women's march was, and that it would certainly succeed in preventing parliament from adopting any laws contrary to sharia.

She was sharing her feelings with a man she'd only ever seen for a few minutes three days earlier in his sister's house – a man who had a violent urge to vomit when he saw the horrible march. Was this really her reason for calling him down from his hotel room?

Maybe she was mad. Maybe she was a strange kind of proselytiser, unafraid of going into a hotel to look for a man she wasn't related to (in a city that criminalised such a thing) just a few metres away from a million Salafi obscurantists filling the streets.

Or maybe she was someone important. A courageous woman whose convoluted calculations and intricate power plays allowed her to do what she wanted.

She had an adventurous streak, that was for sure.

What an incredible city this was, my wretched new capital!

I never hold back when it comes to discussing civil society or debating with Salafis: it's a free for all, all or nothing, life or death.

'I'm shocked by this dark march, and even more so by its obscurantist slogans,' I told her bluntly.

Honestly, more than anything, I was shocked that she was speaking to me from behind a niqab. Before that moment,

I'd never spoken to a woman in a niqab, not once. I didn't think I'd be able to hold a conversation with a shadow.

I had an overwhelming desire to see her face.

'*Istaghfurallah*, God forgive you!' She said. 'Those slogans are verses in the Quran, the word of God Almighty himself! Do you realise what you're saying?'

'Sure, maybe those slogans were advanced for their time – fourteen centuries ago,' I responded hotly. 'But from today's perspective, the women carrying posters with those slogans are slaves, slaves happy with their shackles. They're lacking the sixth sense, the most important one of all: a sense of freedom! Because—'

'There is wisdom in all that God says,' she interrupted softly, forcing me to contain my anger. 'It's wholly forbidden to doubt His word. Sometimes we don't fully understand it, or we don't know how to interpret it. But obeying it, and it alone, is the path to truth and righteousness. I'll pray for God to guide you.'

'—because from a modern perspective the words "and smack them" are an incitement to violence! That's unacceptable in an age of human rights,' I continued.

'What violence? The "smack" mentioned in sharia is educational, done lightly. A beating by which God honours women: without insult or violence. Not with a stick; with a *miswak* for example, nothing more.'

(*A beating by which God honours women.* Amazing! It took a moment to register that I was actually hearing this.)

'People don't brush their teeth with a *miswak* anymore, darling. Do you mean a toothbrush? Or a light smack with a tube of toothpaste?'

I was fond of the word 'darling' (rarely used in Salafi circles). But she didn't like anything that sounded like I was taunting her.

'*Istaghfurallah*, God forgive you!'

I was becoming more and more annoyed talking with this stranger behind a niqab.

'I'm sorry, darling, it's really hard to talk with someone whose face I can't see,' I finally told her.

(You know as well as I do, dear Azazeel, that with people like these, you'll keep chomping at the bit if you don't take the reins.)

She didn't hesitate. In a split second, she'd removed the niqab from her face, right there in the hotel lobby, though she kept her hair completely covered.

Chapter Eight

I started coming to Sana'a during every holiday. I visited at other times as well, for educational and cultural functions organised in coordination with Yemeni universities and cultural bodies.

Four years went by from the first time I saw Ama al-Rahman at my sister's flat to the point when I found my own flat in a family housing complex, which I had finally chosen after much effort. It wasn't far from the city centre, and wasn't so crowded as to rule out the possibility of regular intimate encounters.

I won't trouble you, dear Snatcher of Souls, with the meandering details of my relationship with Ama al-Rahman in the intervening years. I don't have questions for you, but I'd like to say a few things—

'Later, maybe later,' my friend interjects. He always prefers me to cut to the chase.

Well then, dear Wrecker of Delights: we would meet every day in my flat in Sana'a. I don't remember how I spent a single hour of the day before four in the afternoon or after ten at night: all those hours were worthless to me. I waited, bored, as they trudged past – because life, my whole life, began at four o'clock in the afternoon and ended just before ten at night.

These six hours were the hours of Ama al-Rahman's freedom, when she left the special closed complex.

The complex included the palaces of Imam Mohammed al-Hamdani: leader of Yemeni Salafis, and spiritual father of al-Qaeda's first generation of commanders. It also held the palaces of some of his immediate family and other relatives. Most importantly, it included his son Omar's palace. Sheikh Omar was a pampered fool of an imam, whose extremist and obscurantist religious discourse surpassed even that of his father. He didn't have his father's experience, however. Nor his shrewdness or serpent-like qualities.

Ama al-Rahman left the complex on a Salafi mission: to 'champion Faith and Righteousness, and lead the Caliphate State, the State of Islam, to victory.'

She rarely arrived at my flat at four in the afternoon. Usually she came at sunset. She accomplished many things in the two hours she made me spend in torturous anticipation.

She went from one women's qat gathering to another, half an hour here, another there. Laughter, fun, Salafi incitement, religious prayers, organising and drawing people in.

She met throngs of women proselytisers, explained the next day's tasks, followed up with women she'd put in charge of social media, and managed the computers at Piety University. The University was headed by Imam al-Hamdani, and home to covert Salafi and terrorist websites.

She was brilliant in these meetings. Everyone waited for her, enthralled. When it came to managing social relationships, helping others (especially the poor and needy), solving their problems, and bringing them into the fold of the Salafis, she was unparalleled. Not to mention the fact that she was exceptionally beautiful, sexy, and glowed with energy.

Everyone knew she was always on the go, from one appointment to the next. But in between visiting one home and another, she hopped on a public bus that stopped near the gate of the housing complex I lived in.

She arrived at these 'love-ins' (as we both called them) or 'rehearsals for paradise' (as I called them), and we went from the heights of freedom and maddening desire (which would last about an hour) to calm valleys of lounging around (for two hours). We whispered romantically, talked about our days, laughed abundantly, and debated our staunchly opposed intellectual positions (all interspersed, at times, with amorous forays).

Thick blazing love; silent spiritual war.

'Waiting so long makes me ravenous for you,' I told her once.

'Doesn't that make it all the more tantalising, *habibi*?'

'Waiting for you kills me, *qalbi*.'

'Looking forward to sex is life's sweetest suffering, don't you think?'

'I miss you to death when you're not here.'

'I miss you more.'

Then, every time, my spiritual adversary would turn into a physical ally.

No one in the residential complex asked the leader of Yemeni obscurantists what Ama al-Rahman did on any particular day, or whom she visited. It was practically impossible to imagine she wasted a single moment of the time she spent outside the house.

The reason: her ability to mobilise other women, with astounding success. She could organise a march of a million Salafi women, and that was a clear sign she wasn't frittering away the hours. Not to mention her faith, which was beyond reproach. Even beyond Salafi extremism, at times.

Everyone acknowledged that she was the best Islamist proselytiser in Yemen, and a perfect wife (by the laws of God and His Prophet) for Sheikh Omar, the oldest son of a prominent Yemeni religious scholar and the face of obscurantism itself. Her husband's father, however, was more devoted to her (contrary to the laws of God and His Prophet) than he was.

Perhaps when she left the house during those hours, it gave her husband some peace, in one way or another: he closed the door to his palace and engaged in fiqh research and religious activities on the internet, on his famous Facebook page. Or so everyone believed. In reality, he had a very worldly life behind those closed doors: his mistress, and a bottle of the finest whiskey.

Chapter Nine

Ama al-Rahman always showed up eventually, right under the nose of people in the most conservative country in the world.

With microscopic attention, and complete infatuation, I followed her from the moment she stepped off the bus until she knocked on my door.

The strangest thing: the compound office manager and doorman nodded a respectful greeting to her when she arrived. You'd think they would have considered her daily visits to my flat immoral, and that it was their job to prevent a scandal. That was how things normally worked in this arid city, conservative to its marrow.

How did I manage this? How did I justify it? How did she hypnotise them and pull them under her sway? Did she have a flat of her own in the complex? Did she go there when I wasn't around?

I'll never know.

She lay there, liberated, not even wearing her thong. I'd never seen panties like hers in all my life, so skimpy you'd need a microscope to see them. (Where did the Salafis get thongs like these? Did they have their own panty factories, where the same people who spent all day avenging this or that produce lingerie to spite their niqabs? Was this the laudable, pious asceticism they advocated?)

She coyly played with a few qat leaves from time to time, occasionally picking up a few to chew.

I lay stretched out on the bed, naked like she was, my head resting on her waist. With my fingertips I traced her sides, her spine, all her intoxicating curves, slowly, happily. . . we gazed up at the ceiling together, talking, laughing, showering each other with kisses, staring at each other, breathing each other in, talking, laughing more, and more, talking and talking.

Moments of unparalleled joy. Pure, weightless happiness.

I soon learned, dear Wrecker of Pleasures: those two hours were always punctuated by Ama Rahman's little urgent activities. She took calls, responded to texts, and checked the internet.

I soon realised that she was not just the brains behind the Salafi proselytisers, and the motor driving them, but the flame that kept their intensity burning. A black flame, darker than darkness itself.

'Tell me about cultural life in paradise,' I asked her between calls.

'Only God knows what Heaven is like.'

'Are there books there? Are there cultural gatherings in paradise?'

'Only God knows!'

'Are there rivers of milk, and honey, and wine?'

'Of course. There's "what no eye has seen nor ear has heard," as the Hadith says!'

'Have you read *The Epistle of Forgiveness,* by al-Ma'arri, and his description of Heaven and Hell?'

'Do you mean *The Dog's Epistle: Blind Forgiveness*?' She asked scornfully.

'Where did you hear those dirty words?'

'Imam Mohammed al-Hamdani, may God protect him, told me about that rubbish.'

Her phone rang. I listened closely to every word she said. I got to know her, little by little, from tiny fragments of those calls. I was impressed with her. I liked her (loved her, to be honest). I had compassion for her, more and more. I was afraid of her, and hated her too.

'In the Paris metro I saw a girl's severed limbs scattered among charred pencils, after a cowardly terrorist bombing. Is that permitted in Islam?' I asked her.

'Jihad against idolatry is a religious duty. We must avenge our Muslim brothers, because the Jews and Christians spill our blood and rob our land every day.'

'What was that girl guilty of?'

'We're in an eternal war against infidels. It's war, not a game, *habibi*. They kill us however they can, and we do the same.'

'And that image doesn't bother you?'

'You love useless debate, but you're afraid of the actual battlefield.' She paused a moment. 'Why do you always bring that girl up, sweetheart?'

'Not a night goes by without that image pressing down on me like a nightmare. My whole life revolves around it.'

'Oh sweetheart, it kills me to hear that. Read the Quran before you go to sleep so nightmares can't get near you. Don't forget to say the prayer that dispels nightmares before you go to sleep, to protect yourself from them – and the prayer for nightmares if they still manage to get to you.'

I said nothing.

(I stared at the ceiling. It read my thoughts and absorbed my feelings. I remembered the prayers written all over my sister's walls, the prayer for almonds and pistachios, and all kinds of prayers to dispel nightmares.)

'I love you to death, *habibi*,' she said.

'I love you more, *hayati*: I love you to the death of death.'

Chapter Ten

There were two hours between four in the afternoon and the moment Ama al-Rahman knocked on my door, dear Reaper. I always took a short nap (while my internal clock fluttered), and then observed a special ritual. I recall the particulars often, oddly enough.

(If the Breaker of Delights and Ender of Desires eagerly joins the conversation and insists I tell the story – because, like me, he can't resist the details – I'll tell him the following.)

At that time of day I was always to be found standing at my little window, looking out through the grillwork at the street and passing cars. I was waiting for Ama al-Rahman to step off the bus, dissolve into the tumult of the street, and confidently head towards the building complex. She wore a loose veil these days. (It enveloped the tighter-fitting veil with buttons I'd seen her wearing at my sister's. A veil, on top of a veil, on top of a veil!) She always carried a bag with a thermos of tea and things for the house.

She looked like an ordinary wife, nothing to set her apart from any other woman, coming home with modesty and dignity.

A sacred, sublime moment I never wanted to miss.

In that hour and a half or two hours I spent glued to the window, I would also look out to the left, at the balcony across from my window. My gaze would slip through the half-open door and into the living room.

The reason: this hour of waiting was also a sacred daily ritual for the short white-haired man who lived next door. He resembled Yitzhak Shamir, but his body was frail. His steps were delicate and he had a delicate build, and seemed to be preparing for some kind of special occasion.

After four in the afternoon, he always emerged from the bathroom on the first floor, having trimmed his beard with noticeable care. He would walk exceptionally slowly through his living room, even though he can't have been older than sixty-five.

He would dress in front of the full-length mirror, preparing for his own personal moment in history.

He would put on trousers and a matching jacket, usually green, with a smart white shirt. He would put on a red tie, also slowly (he was the only man in Sana'a who wore a tie in those days, particularly in working class neighbourhoods). He always tied it carefully, with exceptional concentration.

He would examine himself in the mirror several times, and go out onto the balcony once or twice, looking for something. From my window, I could just about make out his wife and a few relatives crossing the room to offer him a tissue or sock.

This ritual always lasted a long time. I would peer out and reflect on what I could see. It was quite clear the man wasn't going to a qat gathering. He wasn't dressed in the working-class clothes typical of those get-togethers, but in the suit of an office manager or prominent civil servant.

Then the door on the ground floor of his house would open. His wife would douse him with cologne in the doorway, then he would say goodbye to her, whom I only ever notice when he opens the door. He would slowly walk a few metres towards the front gate, hunching over, and then just as slowly, he would open it.

He would lock it behind him, and take a step towards the pavement. Nervous, worried. Two steps. He would look around, in front of him. To him, each step was like a vast ocean.

He would step out onto the pavement at a tortoise's pace, looking around more and more attentively. He would forge on through the commotion and dust, gradually approaching the street, where the cars hurtle past at frantic speed in this city where no one respects red lights.

My neighbour always waited a long time for the approaching traffic to be far enough away for him to cross with slow steps and not be hit by a car. Perpetual fear. Melancholic waiting. Life or death.

I would observe it all, my heart and nerves attuned to him, wondering about the way he moved and looked around. It drew me in, distracted me. Led me across that endless stretch of time while I waited for Ama al-Rahman's bus, and for her to emerge from it.

In the time between every two steps he took, I would watch the rusty roofs of passing cars, the refuse of the city, and all those people: legions of the dispossessed, half-dead, smeared with decay, getting ready for the usual qat gatherings after a quick lunch, slobbering over a handful of leaves in the hours when the city feels charged with electricity.

While watching my neighbour, I often recalled minute details from the four years between the first time I met Ama al-Rahman at my sister's house and our 'rehearsals for paradise'.

She insisted on involving me in the whirlwind that was her life. The way she did it was terribly traditional: temptation, refraining, tears, laughter, dead ends, flirting, half-hearted abstention, quarter-hearted abstention, girlish games, kids' games . . .

She had decided we would end up sleeping together long, long before this (as I later learned).

Most importantly: she brought me into her life as a new contradiction. To balance the old contradictions with more contradictions, just like the mad old Arabic saying goes: 'Cure me with what ails me.'

In the beginning I had reservations. I resisted, worried, hesitated – and then I dashed up the stairs, four at a time. Rushing, struggling, stumbling, loving greedily.

Perhaps I'd been searching for something, many things, and hadn't understood them until now. Searching for myself, first of all, and for deep-reaching roots. Or maybe for Najaa's killer, no more, no less. My killer.

What exactly had I been I searching for, dear Unveiler of Secrets and Revelations?

Was it true that every love fills a certain void, avenging a grief that knows no cure?

My neighbour always managed to cross the road to the pavement on the other side. Right, left. A real tortoise. He would pass a shop selling car tyres, and then one selling juice.

After these came a hectic, dirty petrol station. He would pass it with heightened apprehension and concentration. He would try to avoid the beggars and the other pedestrians jostling around him so they wouldn't touch him and wrinkle the smart, clean suit he'd spent so much time putting on.

Then the third (and the most difficult) stage would come, at the end of his life-or-death loop: crossing the traffic again, from the petrol station to the pavement in front of his house, to end the journey back where he began.

Traffic, chaos: he navigated it silently. He would dissolve into the street, then continue even more slowly. No one would look at him, but he would look into every face, at every detail, large or small. It was as if his mission were to inspect everything passing near him in this rat race that trampled everyone unapologetically.

I always watched him from my window for about half an hour, following him, observing how he negotiated every step. Progressing slowly, pausing often.

He would complete two laps, and then begin the home stretch. He always looked victorious, happy. He'd move away from the boxing ring of the street, closer to home. Returning victorious once again.

I would watch his face as he arrived back from his daily journey, like someone coming home from an arduous voyage around the world. Every step was victorious, a celebration. A wan smile. Deep, profound joy.

He'd approach the gate at the same slow crawl, unlock it hesitantly, with difficulty. I would be watching him, increasingly enraptured.

His wife always greeted him with longing and open arms. They would embrace.

Glory to life!

Glory to life!

At that moment I knew the person I was waiting for would arrive soon. In ten minutes. Twenty. Fifty minutes. No more.

Chapter Eleven

Sometimes Ama Rahman unleashed a torrent of insults on her husband, Imam Omar, during our 'love-ins'. It was the only personal subject she was comfortable opening up to me about. In reality she desperately needed the release. She insulted him in front of me, again and again. Hated him fiercely. Acted to spite him in every moment. Her greatest joy: eternal revenge.

Every moment of her life, everything she did was, in fact, part of that revenge. She avenged herself constantly, for this or that slight with this or that act, although sometimes I didn't know which was which.

I found out from her (perhaps the only real secret she ever revealed to me about her personal life) that he took advantage of her absence to close the door to his room and drink alcohol (his sacred motto: 'whisky, nothing but whisky'), while everyone else thought he was busy with fiqh research.

They had a solemn and inviolable agreement: she told no one about his alcoholism, and he allowed her to spend those six hours however she wanted. He didn't lose sleep over it, not a wink.

His Takfiri campaigns became more zealous during those pious hours (as anyone following his activities on the internet could see). Imam Omar was well-known for berating atheists, communists, and members of civil society (even if they were religious) and declaring them infidels. He was an infidel-proclaiming machine. At least he didn't have his father's cleverness or malicious streak, as Arab presidents and kings' sons in the nineteen-eighties and nineties often did.

'What do you say to Imam Omar about his alcoholism?' I asked her once.

'I tell him: may God give you guidance.'

'How does he respond?'

'May God guide you and us both.'

'May God guide him, you, and us all,' I retort.

'I love you, *omri*.'

'I love you, flame of my heart.'

Aside from insulting Imam Omar, she never uttered a word about her personal life. Especially not about the ambiguous relationship she had with his father.

She vehemently forbade me from even approaching the subject. She shut down my attempt with a dark look if I tried to slip a question in edgewise, or ask how she really felt towards that guru of hers, the magnetic hypnotist. I was afraid of angering her, to be honest, because she was capable of leaving me forever.

It wasn't that I was worried about upsetting her. I was terrified she really would leave me.

I'd grown used to these 'rehearsals for paradise' with Ama al-Rahman, and how wonderful they were: our bond became more intense, deep, and intimate. Our love seemed to grow from seeds planted in a past life.

Our desire became more heightened during those heavenly rehearsals, the long, tender hours of sharing each other's bodies.

We escaped the tragedies of our lives with passionate intensity. Both of us had an innate need for this, in the double lives we'd been handed by fate.

Ama al-Rahman made love with near-spiritual devotion. She closed her eyes most of the time. Murmured occult verses to herself. She came to it like prayer, with complete religious surrender.

Then, when she opened her eyes, she really opened them. In an instant she transformed into a sex kamikaze; a solitary jihadi; an entire bold and reckless army, marching beneath banners that proclaimed something like: 'The sea behind you, passion in front of you, in your arms, inside you, behind you.'

She always took delight in making love, even though it was a risky affair. Not just risky, but truly dangerous: I may as well have been a guest in Bin Laden's house, sleeping with a female captive of his, all just a few kilometres from al-Qaeda headquarters. (Ama al-Rahman was not just a captive, but a gift. A beautiful woman who had fallen from the heavens into the most sacred place in Imam al-Hamdani's heart. She was also his son's wife.)

Nothing disturbed those two tender, happy hours except for a phone call from a hardworking Salafi or proselytiser, on matters of procedure. Ama al-Rahman was an active Salafi leader, and women always sought her opinion and guidance. No one else could direct, instruct, and lead people like she could. She had an unparalleled dynamism, not to mention close ties with a powerful imam.

Even though I didn't hear the conversations, I noticed that Ama al-Rahman excelled at giving quick, practical responses.

She solved organisational problems with just a few simple words and an inimitable ingenuity.

Her calm, confident responses and beautiful religious phrases seemed to match the different voices she used: firm at times, soft at others. It was so different to the voice she used with me, as if she were leading a prayer when she picked up the phone, and not in the midst of a tryst.

Ama al-Rahman had the ability (quite unlike me) to change the tone of her voice in the blink of an eye.

Then the call would end, Ama al-Rahman would forget the conversation completely, and her tone would become light, melodious, full of laughter and passion once again. (Her voice was dazzling, colourful, a rainbow). She committed herself to our heavenly rehearsals with every cell in her body. When the call was over, she would return to what was left of those two hours in which time seemed to stop, and fully dedicate herself to me.

Nothing in life really bothered her, except for the rare phone call from her husband during a whisky-induced fiqh contemplation session.

Perhaps she knew from the flavour of his voice what kind of drunk he was that night. Sometimes it was romantic (obscene drivel in reality; we mocked him mercilessly). Sometimes it was horribly rapacious, especially when he ordered her, in the middle of the call, to come home right then.

She swore about him with the harshest religious curses, often interspersed with the highly romantic phrase *Allah yehraq qalboh* – God burn his heart. Her freedom, in those six hours, was sacred. He had no right to touch her.

These calls occurred every time his good friend, Sheikh Abdul Rahman, came to visit. Sheikh Abdul Rahman was a senior Yemeni sheikh, one of the most vehement opponents to the proposed law against child marriage (Mohammed married Aisha at age nine, he argued). Abdul Rahman often came to spend the day with him, sleep over, and take part in his clandestine whiskey binges. No one in the whole palace knew about it, except for Ama al-Rahman.

Ama al-Rahman hated Sheikh Omar's militaristic orders to come home immediately. To her, the orders violated her implicit pact with him: no one knew he was an alcoholic, and he didn't bother her during those six hours.

Besides, she especially hated seeing Sheikh Abdul Rahman. Just like she hated seeing her husband. Just like she hated her whole life, the endless tragedy she'd been fated to.

The only thing in life she loved, she told me, were those brief hours in bed next to me.

'Since we first met in the blind man's shop, I've never loved anyone else,' she often said.

No one else? I didn't believe it.

'Why not?' The words unexpectedly escape the Reaper's lips, in a moment of curiosity that seems to take him by surprise.

'There was something in her eyes, dear Wrecker of Delights, that betrayed her when she said it, just slightly.'

'Sorry, please go on,' he says, apologising for interrupting.

Ama al-Rahman got really upset whenever her husband called: she knew he never interrupted those six sacred hours (from when he went to sleep until dawn prayers) unless things had got tense between the two alcoholic sheikhs, and they needed her to quickly and discretely intervene.

Sometimes one of them fell down the stairs, or they began a duet of vomiting and couldn't stop.

The strange thing was that when this happened, she didn't leave my flat and run to catch to the first taxi home to rescue the drunkards.

No. Instead, something very strange would happen, to my sole benefit and utter delight.

She had a desire to avenge her husband's calls (she lived by a philosophy of revenge, constantly avenging this or that) and retaliate against his orders that she come home immediately. (These dampened her spirits and clouded the sweetest hours of her day, she said.) So, each time he ordered her to come back before her six hours of freedom were up, she'd ask me to get the mirror. She'd tell me to put it on the bed, in different places, so we could try different positions she usually thought were too difficult or impossible, the ones she didn't like and always preferred to put off for another time.

After just half an hour of this blessed revenge, I would be trembling at her genius and highly acrobatic sexual positions. The mirror added an element of complexity, creativity, and novelty.

She insisted that we watch ourselves in the mirror. We got off on it, and on watching ourselves watching, too.

She avenged herself fiercely; her lust overwhelmed me. Avenging, growing more aroused, avenging.

I always looked forward to phone calls from Sheikh Omar during his occasional meetings with Sheikh Abdul Rahman in Imam Muhammad's palace complex. I experienced new kinds of pleasures in the half hour in which she avenged him.

Our desperate love-making gained new depths and dimensions I anticipated eagerly.

Blessed religious hypocrisy and flagrant existential contradictions!

Then she'd leave me for the two sheikhs. Who knew what kind of state she'd find them in. She enjoyed her revenge, but I enjoyed it even more.

Chapter Twelve

Perhaps inside every Salafi woman sleeps a wolf, hungry for sex. An octopus with seventy arms, each arm a houri. Perhaps, perhaps.

Or perhaps Ama al-Rahman simply fled to the paradise of our sweet, tender love to forget something. Assault, perhaps. Rape.

To avenge something I knew nothing about, through the pure feelings, deep kisses, noble outpourings of emotion, and abounding revelations of our lovemaking.

All I knew was that for our relationship to continue, it had to remain completely secret.

'Would you give me your phone number?' I asked her once, as we began our rehearsals for paradise.

'That's just not possible, *habibi*.'

'You've got two mobiles; I just need the number of one, to send you messages every so often.'

'There's no need, *habibi*.'

'You'd rather an old-fashioned letter then?'

'No, sweetheart.'

'But how will you know when I'm coming to Sana'a?'

'Through your sister, of course.'

Ama al-Rahman might have been the only beloved in the world to refuse all phone calls from her lover. All texts messages, real letters (on paper), any evidence of me whatsoever.

For simple security reasons? Maybe, I don't know.

For deep philosophical reasons? Maybe, maybe. After all, eternal love leaves no trace.

For hidden romantic reasons? Maybe, who knows.

Perhaps passion is dispelled by frequent text messages and phone calls. Perhaps they drain it of romantic yearning and physical desire, as if there were a mathematical equation: the quantity of passion (P) multiplied by the frequency of texts (T) equals a constant (C).

$$P \times T = C$$

An increase in either variable on the left side of the equation (P or T) necessarily decreases the amount of the variable on the right side of the equation (C).

Perhaps, perhaps . . . perhaps this explains the scant number of letters exchanged by a historical couple who stayed in love for their whole lives: Jenny and her husband, Karl Marx. (He signed his letters to her with a code name: *the Moor*, a reference to his light copper skin, apparently.)

Yes, yes. Because every time I was about to return to Sana'a from Paris, I became infatuated with Ama al-Rahman. All day and all night, I thought of nothing but being back in her arms, so warm and white and soft; her scent, which wrapped itself around me all day; and her skin, so smooth and supple and tender. I was dying to touch and stroke and lick her forever.

I came back to Sana'a for two or three weeks several times a year.

And every time, we began our rehearsals for paradise anew, starting from my first day back. A feverish embrace, bodies entwined for hours. (For Salafi women, sex is a sacred ritual. Glory be to Salafi women!)

Then we'd chat in bed. Two naked bodies in blissful, utter abandon. There's nothing in the world so idyllic.

In the years that followed, our hours of lounging around were punctuated by new habits: Ama al-Rahman would go to her handbag and dig around for her laptop – always the latest and lightest MacBook.

This girl who wore veil over veil over veil when she stepped off the bus always walked around the flat naked.

When she was out: layers of veils, one on top of the next. Camouflage to mislead the enemy. She changed the outer veil she had on when she arrived for a different one when she left.

With me: she was as pure as a mountain spring. She flaunted her spellbinding body, celebrated its honest, almost mystical beauty. Incredibly lithe, perfectly proportioned: the waist of a fairy, flowing into sensuous curves. She was endlessly alluring and arousing.

She would lie down with her sleek silver Mac on her chest, just below her breasts. She loved to show off how perfect they were, right down to her pert nipples.

She would interrupt our beautiful hours of lying around in conversation to use the internet on her MacBook, but only for half an hour, at most. (Her mobile phone was connected to a satellite network.) She had to let fellow Salafis (or someone) know she was online, on Facebook, engaged in the struggle, somewhere.

'Does the imam use Facebook?' I asked her.

'Yes.'

'Don't the porn ads on the side bother him?'

'He doesn't look at them.'

'Is using the Internet, and Facebook and Google, permissible according to sharia?'

'Of course. Anything that helps you spread the word of God is not only permissible, but a duty. But you'd be better served by religious websites, *habibi*. They'll help lead you to the path of truth and righteousness.'

'Do you think I should make a Facebook account?'

'No, darling.'

'Why not?'

'Everything you'd write would undermine our faith! It would only serve the idolaters and the misguided. We're in a daily war with them which spares no one.'

I watched her using the internet, not doing much of note. Briefly responding to emails. Clicking between different pages on Facebook. A comment here, another one there.

Sending links for lectures on YouTube, or links to important Salafi websites.

I memorised the names of some of the sites (which masqueraded as ordinary sites, of course) that she commented on (using a fake name, of course). She usually went by 'Jihad Abdel Haq', and sometimes just by 'Ama al-Rahman', not her full name.

A niqab over a niqab. Quicksilver over quicksilver.

'What would happen if your husband or his father found out about this flat?'

'They'd burn us here together. Right on the spot, over a slow and excruciating fire. A beautiful end for two old lovers, don't you think *habibi*?' she added with a slight smile.

'Why don't you run away and come live with me abroad?'

'I'd be too homesick, darling.'

'What if I moved here to Sana'a, would you leave them for me?'

'No.'

'Didn't you tell me that you hate your husband more than any woman has ever hated her husband?'

'I do. But I'm loyal to his father. I won't disappoint my saviour, the apple of my eye . . . May God keep him.'

'After all the years we've been together, and in love, you still haven't cut off your quasi-romantic relationship with him?'

'I've tried! But what can I do? He won't have it!'

Words caught in my throat. Blood boiled in my veins (and in my brain), fuelled by this guru who had hypnotised her since she first laid eyes on him. An obscurantist terrorist charlatan, whose lectures inspired all sorts of murderers, especially suicide bombers.

She noticed my shock, and tried to mollify me.

'It's just a loving relationship with a spiritual father!"

But what can I do? He won't have it, she'd said.

I contemplated this phrase. You'd need a room full of psychologists to unpack it.

How had this monster brainwashed her? How had she become a breeding ground for such contradictions? How could I bear to stay with her and these vexations, which were enough to drive anyone crazy in five minutes?

The truth was that even despite all that, I couldn't leave this succubus. I'd been stung. I really loved her: all the little things about her, her beauty and madness, like glowing lava from a volcano of contradictions. She was my life's new tragedy: my Hawiya, my abyss, and my vertigo as I tumbled downwards.

Oh God, what to do?

I constantly repeated to myself: the only way out was to snatch her from this fishing net, from the claws of her guru sheikh. 'God damn him! And angels and devils damn him too,' as my Grandmother Noor would say.

But every time I came anywhere close to bringing him up, Ama al-Rahman snapped at me.

'How many times have I told you? Don't talk about him, don't mention his name.'

And with the fierceness of an injured wolf, and a dark glare that frightened me, she would stand up to leave the flat, and me, forever.

I'd beg her to stay, and promise I wouldn't mention his name again.

Then I'd return to Paris, where nightmares of the guru, visions of Ama al-Rahman, and memories of Najaa all swirled together. Wherever I went, whatever I did, they never left me. Not for a moment.

Torture, death. Every day I waited to return to Ama al-Rahman and our love-ins. They revitalised me.

So finally, my pressing question for you, dear Breaker of Desires: what heinous crime had I committed against the universe? What act sent my life spinning down this deadly whirlpool?

Chapter Thirteen

I took refuge in Facebook every time I returned to Paris from Sana'a. I wallowed on the site, searching for every word Ama al-Rahman and her fake identities wrote. I browsed the pages of her army of fellow Salafis and followers, her insane husband, and his father the fanatical Yemeni imam. All the tentacles of their obscurantist networks.

Just like her, I created a Facebook account under a fake name: mine was Mushtaq Abd al-Bari (al-Ramdani.) I had added 'al-Ramdani' in the hope that it would seem more like a real name.

I tried to add Ama al-Rahman and Jihad Abdul Haq as friends. Neither accepted me. Maybe because they each had five thousand Facebook friends (*mufaysbookeen*, as they say in Yemen: Facebookites), which was the maximum. So I became just one more of Ama al-Rahman's 12,335 official followers, and Jihad Abdul Haq's 27,883 official followers.

What did I see? Thousands of likes and commenters on every post she wrote. I don't think she read them all. There were so many, and most of what they wrote was brief and inconsequential.

I joined the fray, and commented on everything Ama al-Rahman wrote. Most of the time from a very secular point of view, against what she posted, but in highly literary and respectful language. I tried not to sound like I did in our conversations in Sana'a, so she wouldn't suspect who I was. I didn't want to be exposed.

She never liked a single one of my comments. A drove of fellow Salafis often responded though, usually rudely. They took pleasure in quick, cheap insults. I still haven't really registered them.

I'd seen some of their names on her MacBook screen during our 'rehearsals for paradise' in Sana'a, while I secretly watched her doing the rounds on the internet, quickly and cautiously.

I followed this flock's daily online activities. (The 'insult factory', I called them.) Eventually, I realised that most were officially employed in Salafi and extremist networks. They managed hundreds of social media pages, Facebook groups (both open and closed), listservs, and applications that automatically posted religious passages on all their personal Facebook pages every few hours.

Highly organised clandestine work. Fake names everywhere. Armies of darkness. Salafi jihad, armed with the latest technology and antediluvian rhetoric.

Distant centuries burst into laughter.

They often rallied to comment on my secular posts, and attacked me when I called for freedom of conscience and thought. They worked to frustrate people who wrote posts like mine, and to provoke and pressure them. Sometimes they even launched collective attacks to get the Facebook administration to close the person's account. (*The air of Hell is too thick for hymns!*). This was alongside their secret online terrorist activities, of which I noticed countless hints here and there.

Intense online struggle. Legions of Salafis on a supposedly secular platform.

Perpetual spiritual combat, no less brutal than conventional war.

I was active on Facebook, my posts were clear and well written, and soon I had five thousand Facebook friends. I accepted friend requests with hardly a thought.

I realised much later, when I clicked on their profiles to read what they posted, that 4,700 of them were either morons, obscurantists, lovers of tyranny, or thugs.

Intentionally or not, together they formed an army – whether virtually or in real life – rallying behind my lover. If not exactly an army, at least devoted admirers of her page.

Every time I wrote a short post, I had to control my temper at the responses, and patiently continue with my enlightened discourse. I didn't beat about the bush, and didn't give in to their provocations, insults, or flippant comments. Not even when they called me a criminal.

Writing around them, dear Azazeel, was like walking on eggshells.

'That's old news,' says my friend, surprising me with his interjection. 'Darkness is naturally hostile to the light, and naturally, zealously, seeks to extinguish it.' Then he asks me not to respond to what he said, as he can see he's interrupted my train of thought. 'I'm sorry, please go on,' he adds.

I believed what my friend said. I had to make a constant effort to explain what I was saying to people who seemed semi-illiterate at times; whatever I said, they took the exact opposite from it. Idiots who 'look at your finger when you're pointing to

the moon,' as the well-known Chinese expression goes. I don't
how anyone can hold a conversation with them.

I regularly made sure to post links of my conversations with
other Facebook users on Ama al-Rahman's pages, trying to catch
her attention. I hoped she would read them and be provoked into
engaging in a conversation with me directly. I'd learned from my
conversations with 'the herd', and had systematically developed
my responses.

Ama al-Rahman never engaged in discussion with me,
though. She didn't comment on any of my comments on her
pages, or the links I posted there.

Slowly but surely my Facebook page increased in popularity,
thanks primarily to the attentions of my opponents. Some
considered the page as 'daily enlightenment'; they thought I was
'a real straight talker', 'someone who isn't afraid of the truth', as
they put it.

The obscurantists' attacks increased as well. My page was shut
down several times by Facebook as a result of their collective
complaints, even though it was clearly a model of respect for
freedom of expression and opinion. I always discussed things
politely, and was careful not to hurt anyone.

I'd once seen Ama al-Rahman send a brief message to a group
of militants: 'Please report this page. It insults the True Religion
and Khadija, Mother of Believers, peace be upon her.'

I noticed the message while sitting next to her, flipping
through a newspaper or book (which I'd do whenever she opened
her MacBook). She was never bothered that I occasionally
glanced at her screen. It didn't trouble her, and she never turned
the screen away, or at least only rarely. It was as if she had a

religious conviction that sooner or later I would join her war: a war of truth, faith, and salvation.

I later checked the page she'd wanted to ban. I didn't see anything insulting Khadija, nothing I considered 'an insult to the True Religion.' Not even remotely.

Eons of my Facebook life passed, dear Reaper, before I saw a comment from Jihad Abdul Haq responding to a short post I had made.

I rubbed my hands in delight at how long I'd waited for that moment. I was prepared. (Perhaps, somehow, it liberated me from my lust.)

This is how our conversation went, dear Reaper, down to the letter, no narrative interventions or editorial alterations:

Post on my Facebook wall:

After the West separated religion from schools, politics, and public life, modern society developed in every regard. (Western civilisation also completely respects religion as an individual spiritual activity, something personal and private.)

Jihad Abdul Haq's response:

Things in Islamic countries are different to Christian and Jewish countries. We don't separate religion from politics and education, as enemies of God and Islam want us to.

Thanks to religion, we expanded into China and Southern
Spain. All scientific advancements in Islamic societies
happened in a religious context.

Mushtaq Abd al-Bari (al-Ramdani), in a comment:

Their religion conquered the world too, dear Jihad, and
still has followers from the Americas to Australia. They
developed numerous scientific inventions in the context
of their religion (that is, when it played a dominant role in
their lives), from the telescope to electricity. Meanwhile we
didn't invent anything of note, not even at the height of our
civilisation, aside from perhaps improving on the ancient
Chinese astrolabe.

Yet despite this, today they ban religion from interfering in
education and politics.

Of course, we produced great thinkers and philosophers, like
Abul 'Ala al-Ma'arri, who were centuries ahead of the rest of
world. But we persecuted them, and even today we haven't
learned from what these great pioneers accomplished.

Jihad:

God honoured us alone with Islam. Not them!

Mushtaq:

Clearly! Don't you see we're wallowing in a pit of
backwardness? We've been fighting in the name of religion
for centuries, hurtling towards the ruinous depths of the
world, deafened by the thunder of our successive defeats.

Jihad:

The blame lies not with Islam, but with non-practicing
Muslims.

Mushtaq:

After so many centuries of failure, how are things supposed
to change? I doubt that creating a new righteous, pious
Ummah - one that understands what our priests want, and
puts that into practice - is possible.

In their eyes it's not their mythology, teachings, and mind-
numbing, antiquated laws that are to blame, but us fools. We
only study religious history, and are then shaped in its image.
We see life and the universe only through their perspective,
we learn only what their teachings have approved (their

sharia laws, which punish or annihilate anyone who opposes them). In their eyes, our fundamental problem is that we too were created from Adam's crooked rib!

(The opening moves in the chess game were over, dear Snatcher of Souls. Now it was war!)

Jihad (dryly and dismissively):

You don't understand anything! You use words like 'priests' that have nothing to do with our religion. Before these 'centuries of failure', as you say, we were one of the most advanced civilisations in the world, thanks to God's will and our practicing the teachings of Islam. By implementing the teachings of Islam, and with God's will, we can again lead the world.

Mushtaq:

You may as well be talking about an organism who never evolved out of the primordial soup, but who won't stop going on about his past glory. He looks at the dinosaurs with their wings and fins, the beasts who now rule the land, seas, and sky, and says: 'Nyah, nyah! Back when we were both single cell organisms, I was the stronger one!'

It's true we were at the forefront of the world in the Middle
Ages (during the Umayyad and Abbasid periods). If time had
stopped then, we'd still be leaders of the world.

Our problem is that time didn't stop, and those who don't
keep up with history are left behind.

Centuries have passed, my dear, (since Galileo's telescope,
the Enlightenment, and the modern age). In that time,
their mentality has developed into what you see today.
Meanwhile, ours hasn't changed.

We're still single cell organisms, while Western organisms
(who once really were weaker than us), have evolved fins
and wings, and now rule the universe.

Fins and wings = not being bound to unscientific axioms.

Production of knowledge today differs to that of the past
(a past we haven't been able to leave behind).

Modern fins and wings include:

Scientific proof (as opposed to supposed revelations by God);

Tangible experience;

Space for questioning and doubt, that isn't restricted by
religious red lines;

Differentiating between religious history and scientific history, between religious axioms and scientific truths. Not treating religious axioms as if they were scientific truths (from the creation of the world in six days, to Eve being created from Adam's rib, the apple, the expulsion from paradise. Modern science completely contradicts these obsolete beliefs).

Jihad (quite angry and agitated):

Listen here: you are challenging our religion, beliefs, and way of life. God forgive you for straying from what is right. I'll pray for God to guide you.

Mushtaq:

I'm sorry dear Jihad: I'm speaking to you in mathematical language, and you're responding with apostasy. Let me know when you're ready to have a rational discussion based on the facts.

(She didn't respond. Maybe she was trying to calm herself down. Of course, I knew that thousands of her followers were reading every word of our discussion. Her admirers and supporters flocked to her comments with hundreds of likes. None of my comments had more than seven likes, from seven shy secularists who hid behind seven fake identities. I called them the 'seven honourable sons'.

I didn't expect Jihad to continue the discussion after that last comment, but she returned with a fierce and strategic offensive.)

Jihad:

> Learn about your own religion before discussing it, you idiot! Our faith accepts questioning and inquiry. Al-Ramadi, you're arguing over something you know nothing about!

> Take the stories of those prophets who used questioning and inquiry, like Prophet Ibrahim, peace be upon him. At first, Ibrahim looked up at the stars and said 'This is my Lord'. Then eventually he arrived at the truth and became a believer in God.

(The debate got better, dear Stealer of Spirits; the game was in full swing. These people use stories however it suits them, generalising and rewriting history as they see fit. I wouldn't let them get away with it!)

Mushtaq:

> We're not talking about the same kind of investigation here, dear Jihad. Scientific examination is different. It

doesn't just accept God's supposed revelations as the truth. For example: from a scientific point of view, Prophet Ibrahim isn't a historical figure. Neither is Prophet Moses. There isn't a single piece of scientific evidence that he existed, aside from being mentioned in the Torah. According to religious history, the Torah was revealed on Mount Sinai to Moses himself, on panels written by the God of the children of Israel, in the twelfth century BC.

But scientific history uses Carbon–14 analysis to date paper and stone, and modern methods to analyse the history of words and the origins of texts. After two centuries of scientific research, it was determined that the Torah was written by more than sixty people (most notably Ezra, a prominent rabbi who lived in Babylon during the migration and diaspora), in different languages. It was based on ancient Jewish rabbinical tradition, and taken from the texts of previous civilisations and beliefs, some time between the fourth and the seventh century BC. It's mostly filled with myths unconfirmed by science, like the war between Moses and the Pharaoh, and other fantastical tales with no foundation in reality.

Do you accept this kind of scientific investigation?

Jihad (who was beginning to lose her temper, and resorted to a skirmish before suicide-bombing the chess king):

First of all: Your name means 'The Creator', Mr. al-Bari. But do you even believe in God? Are you even a Muslim?

('Wow,' my dear friend, the Reaper, laughs wryly. I laugh too. 'What a comment! Stunning intellectual depth, and exemplary argumentative abilities!' Still, her comment got 971 likes. Maybe it was the lion's last roar before going in for the kill.)

Mushtaq (who was used to this sort of attack in his daily discussions with her herd of followers):

A question straight out of the Middle Ages! We live in the age of 'freedom of conscience' (in other words: the freedom to believe in religion, or not to believe, or to change your beliefs as you like). One's beliefs (or lack thereof) are a matter for the private sphere. Here on Facebook we're in the public sphere, and we talk about issues for the public sphere.

It's like asking 'What's your blood type?': these are personal questions that don't belong in a secular public space.

Jihad:

There's no hope for you! You want us to doubt our faith, which is complete, infallible, and all-encompassing? The Almighty said,

'Today I have perfected your religion;
I have completed My bounty upon you;
And I have sanctioned Islam as your religion.'

(The discussion was approaching its climax, dear Snatcher of Souls.
We were almost at checkmate . . . You know better than I do that
these people have a fundamentally antagonistic relationship with the
concept of time. If time were a man, they'd kill him. Maybe they were
vaccinated against the concept of time, or had a natural immunity to
it, like insane people. Here was my big chance: bringing sweet little
Jihad face to face with the fourth dimension: time. Right?)

Mushtaq (Curtly, copying several ready-made phrases and
examples from an article of his. He reveals the emperor's new
clothes for what they are, he launches a thousand temporal
attacks before Jihad has time to draw her sword. He feels they're
nearing the end of this legendary discussion, which a large
number of Facebookites are following):

Perhaps the root of the issue, dear Jihad, is how you interpret
the verse. Honestly, this kind of interpretation is why we're
stuck in the past.

Here's an example: Islam's stance on slavery.

Islam doesn't explicitly forbid slavery like it forbids eating
pork, yet it does encourage people to free slaves.

This was wonderful, and ahead of its time in the sixth century AD, when the great prophet Mohamed lived. But our morals haven't progressed since then.

From then until 1948 (when the UN imposed the Charter of Human Rights, thanks to the West), not a single Muslim thinker, ruler, or jurist called for abolition – in societies filled with slaves and servants, where inequality flourished. Meanwhile, in the West, the seeds were sown for the abolition of slavery in the eighteenth century, the century of enlightenment!

I doubt that keeps zealots like you up at night. But what makes me lose sleep is that for fourteen centuries, not a single Muslim called for the abolition of slavery! They said sharia was 'complete' and didn't need to be amended.

I can't help but notice, darling, that you refuse to admit that the world has changed over the centuries. Here's an example to show you how important this is:

If al-Qaeda (with its jihadi ideas and theories, its current policies, and its Taliban-like organisation) had been founded fourteen centuries ago, it would have been the pinnacle of human civilisation at the time. Its leaders would have been akin to the Prophet's companions or the Rashidun caliphs.

But in the age of human rights, it's a terrorist organisation, unparalleled in its ability to spread ignorance, backwardness, and destruction. Its leaders have no place in our world today; they're no more than killers and criminals.

Jihad (crossly – she'd lost her temper when my words rained down on her skull like a rock avalanche. It was only natural; the concept of time never enters Salafis' minds, they simply can't stand it. They drew their swords when they saw her type the phrase):

You're an infidel, an atheist, and an enemy of God! What do you say, guys?

Mushtaq (angry and provoked. She'd taken out the big guns with the phrase 'enemy of God'. And with 'What do you say, guys?' she'd rallied her Facebook flock to intervene in what should have been a two-player chess match. I decided to aim where I knew it would hurt: Imam al-Hamdani):

You're right: I'm in a daily battle with the god that al-Qaeda, the obscurantists, and Imam al-Hamdani believe in!

But the god of al-Hallaj, Ibn Arabi, and Abu al-Ma'arri – that god I love deeply.

Go on, dearest, tell me: which god are you referring to?

'What do you say, guys?' That's what Jihad Abdul Haq resorted to, letting dozens of fierce tafkiri voices fly.

My page was attacked, in an onslaught of extremist comments, fatwas, and insults, some of them shockingly obscene. Then Facebook disabled my account, permanently this time. I opened a new account, with a new fake name.

If I hadn't mentioned their great leader, Sheikh al-Hamdani, who'd revealed to them the secrets of the unknown, maybe they would have been less vicious.

And if Mushtaq Abd al-Bari (al-Ramdani) hadn't been a fake name, or if they'd discovered my address, I would have been dragged through the streets!

Chapter Fourteen

Post on my wall on Facebook:

There are poems of sadness over Yemen's decline, and poems of nostalgia for the Aden of earlier days, but I've always been drawn to a tragic poem by Ahmed Ali Abdellah. It's called 'Young Abdelrahim', and tells the story of a young man from Aden. He was first swept along by the revolutionary wave of the 1970s and 80s, when Aden was known as 'the beacon of scientific socialism' in the Arab world. Then, after the 1994 Yemeni Civil War, when Aden was occupied and South Yemen became no more than war booty for the victorious Northern tribes, he was dragged down by the Salafi obscurantist tide. He turned into another person: one obsessed with the coming of the Mahdi.

One day (buckle up, now!), Abdelrahim dreamed the sky asked him to murder his eldest son just before dawn prayer. With this Ibrahim-like sacrifice, Abdelrahim himself would become the Mahdi.

So, at call to prayer on a dark dawn in the middle of the 1990s in defeated South Yemen, Abdelrahim woke his eldest son. He took him to pray the dawn prayer at a mosque near their house. Then, at the door to the mosque, he planted a blind shot in his son's skull.

The reverberations of that tragic day still shake Abdelrahim's neighbours' houses and the nearby streets.

The reason: Abdelrahim wakes up every day just before the dawn call to prayer, a fierce nightmare bearing down on him. He screams. Shaking and sobbing, he cries out for his lost son (the echoes shake the street, before merging with the call to prayer). But his son has passed away, and crossed far into the land of Ibrahim's ram and the Mahdi's battles.

Awaking before the call to dawn prayer
Young Abdulrahim's voice is set to shake the nearby soil
Around him, the minarets burst into song
What sound soars louder than voices raised in prayer?

Young Abdelrahim's first child fell victim to modern Yemen's obscurantist ideas. Then 'in a single autumn', his second son falls victim too. 'Sheikh' Abdelrahim's tragedy doubles, in a new form, but one no less disastrous.

In a single autumn, years pass
Red lust befalls the land, on soldiers' heels.

Abdelrahim's second son fell victim to North Yemen's brutal soldiers as they gunned down young men in South Yemen's peaceful resistance, two years before the Arab Spring. This was the beginning of a revolutionary uprising against Saleh -'the Snake'- and his whole regime. The poet narrates the boy's demise:

As the earth is ablaze
In a frenzy of their bullets
Another boy killed
His blood spills
At their feet
The lad slumps
In a swarm of bullets
Abdelrahim keens
Over his son
Bearing his remains.

'A man who's never made secret love to a Salafi woman has never made love at all.' From the moment my rehearsals for paradise with Ama al-Rahman began, I believed this line I'd once read to be true.

It was strange, and truly wonderful: a Salafi woman, when making love, seems to be avenging herself on every taboo, repressed desire, and red line. As if she were actually bound by her religion (as I said earlier) to be seventy houris in a single bed.

Glory to Salafi sex and mad lust!

Clandestine sex with this section of humanity can quickly lead you into a quagmire, though.

That's what happened to me, at least, the day I discovered Ama al-Rahman's parallel relationship. Something more than 'just a loving relationship with a spiritual father':

It felt like being stabbed in the back.

(I fall silent. I take a deep breath before continuing to tell the Angel of the Dead this bitter, exhausting tale.)

'Well then?' My friend sharply interrupts me, with evident curiosity.

(Maybe I confused him with my useless theorising about Jenny and Karl Marx's love letters several minutes ago, and wasted precious time.)

I continue.

Ama al-Rahman didn't tell me when we first started seeing each other, or all at once. She waited (this is what was so difficult to bear) until I'd been stung by her love, until it burrowed into the marrow of my bones; until I was addicted to our rendezvous, unable to live without them.

She waited until my whole life spun in orbit around her, until it was impossible to end things. She was crying that day, several years after our rehearsals for paradise had begun, when she dropped the bomb:

'The truth is, I'm doubly in love. I'm in love with you, and with someone I haven't told you about.'

I almost succumbed to the shock. Or maybe I did succumb to the shock, and still haven't recovered.

'Who is he?'

'Imam Mohamed al-Hamdani.'

I asked a rather stupid question, almost automatically. It didn't really deserve a response.

'Your husband's father?'

She said nothing. I attempted to regain my composure, tried to breathe, and asked another question, a better one this time:

'Didn't you tell me before that it was just a loving relationship with a spiritual father?'

'It's nothing more than that.'

I shuddered. A bottomless abyss. I choked on my words.

'He's not a threat to you now,' she continued calmly and assuredly, as if my brain hadn't just exploded. 'I'm bound to him by love alone; we don't have a physical relationship anymore.'

And just like that, the greatest jinn of them all, Imam Mohamed al-Hamdani, crashed through the ceiling and into my life.

Then, as if we had just concluded a party meeting or press conference, she asked matter-of-factly, 'Do you have any questions, comments, or observations?'

A thousand and one questions collided with each other in the whirlpool she'd thrown me into. The quagmire.

I needed time to take in what she was saying.

The greasy cogs of my brain slowly started to turn. Then they stopped. I should have said something like, 'Give me a minute to put my thoughts together,' but instead I was petrified. Maybe I wanted to save her from this predicament, if she actually thought it was a predicament. At any rate, she seemed unhappy with this long discussion.

I put my head in my hands.

'No, I don't know.'

She took advantage of my response and ended the discussion, pre-empting anything else I could have said.

'Promise me you'll let it go, now that I've told you. And that you won't mention the Imam's name again.'

(In other words: sure, you feel like you've fallen into a trap. But let your jealousy and rejection swell, silently filling your subconscious, until you suffer a sudden heart attack. Or your blood pressure rises until your arteries burst. Or your emotions explode out of you in a tsunami of insanity. Or you throw yourself from the ninetieth floor of the nearest building.)

'I promise.'

I signed my life away. I agreed to enter a prison I couldn't leave. A room without air.

Of course, this name didn't belong to just anyone: it was her husband's father. This was the man who had chosen her to marry his son (for reasons that seemed quite innocent at the time). A man thirty years her senior, so ugly, so repugnant, that angels and even devils despised him.

An obscurantist octopus, a man who definitely had longstanding ties to al-Qaeda terrorists. (Tapes of his religious speeches were popular in Islamic circles, especially in Algeria.) A man responsible for killing Najaa, indirectly, or maybe even directly!

All my loathing poured into him and doubled. I felt sorry for his son, the young Imam. I knew how much Ama al-Rahman hated him. I was sure she'd long since turned down his advances, and would never go near him again. (He had other wives anyway, and many children with them).

Dearest Reaper, I admit: in my tragicomic hysteria, there were times I considered going to Imam Omar to complain about his father. I imagined myself saying tearfully, 'Your wife's cheating on me with your dad!'

I couldn't stop thinking about my adversary, but I didn't talk to Ama al-Rahman about their relationship. I'd promised her I wouldn't. And besides, I knew it would bother her.

Whenever I alluded to this parallel relationship, her gaze calcified (despite quivering slightly).

'I told you everything, isn't that enough?' She'd lash out. 'Didn't you promise you wouldn't bring it up again? Or do you get some underhand pleasure from talking about it?'

My dear friend the Reaper (who, as I've noticed, loves a bit of word play), interrupts.

'"Underhand pleasure". Hah!'

Yes, my dear friend, how those words stung, how wonderful they were: offence and defence at the same time. (They drove themselves into the fibre of my being like a razor.)

Much later, I dared to ask her again, hoping their romance had ended, and become just a friendship, 'But do you still love him?'

Her response was an epic slap to the face.

'It's love, eternal love,' she told me angrily. 'I can't control how I feel about him. But don't worry, we haven't had a physical relationship since you and I started meeting here in the flat, if that's what you're worried about.'

'And him, he loves you?'

'I'm the light of his life, the height of his desires, the one and only woman in his eyes. He begins each day and ends every night, by repeating these words three times: 'I love you by God and through God, I love no one but you, my only desire, my heart and soul, Ama al-Rahman.'

'And you have no intention of ending the relationship. Even though you've told me you love me?'

Terrible silence. Then she added, with words that destroyed me like none other ever had, spoken in the local dialect that pierced me to the core, 'What can I do? He won't have it.' I nearly wanted those words to be the title of this novel, they affected me so much.

They overwhelmed me for what felt like several minutes.

'And how do you respond when he professes his love three times?' I finally asked.

'I say, "You're my only love, may God keep you and care for you." I say it three times too,' she responded. (She who had long professed that I was the only one she loved, since passion had first pulsed through her heart.)

And I thought God cursed all liars!

She saw my jaw quiver and my eyelids flutter.

'It's just something we say out of habit. He's not a threat to you, I've told you a thousand times.'

She noticed all the colours of the rainbow cross my face at once. My eyes went as red as if they were about to burst out bleeding, and she tried to reassure me.

'He asked me to sleep with him again, like we used to . . . but this time I said no.'

What reassurance! My horror grew at this fearful adversary of mine – my *tabeen*, you could say (the male form of the word *tabeena*, which in Yemeni dialect means sister-wife). My brother-husband!

I was drowning in a swamp, and could do nothing to escape.

Then she repeated her warning that I was not to mention his name again, nor ask her any more questions about him. Otherwise . . .

From the moment Hawiya first came to the hotel lobby to look for me in the summer of 1996, dear Snatcher of Souls, I grew accustomed to the dictatorial nature of this threat.

I still haven't told you everything that happened that day. A strange explosion, the Big Bang itself.

Back in the hotel lobby, after our debate about *The sharia permits four wives* (and the rest of the slogans from that protest march) had intensified, I told her, 'I'm sorry, darling, I find it really hard to talk with someone when I can't see her face.'

And she didn't hesitate. In a split second she'd removed the niqab from her face, right there in the hotel lobby, though she kept her hair completely covered.

The greatest surprise was that this young woman, with a pure Sana'a accent, looked surprisingly like the girl from the blind man's shop.

The more I looked at her, the more dumbfounded I was by the similarities.

I noticed that she was no less confused.

A long silence; descending in tandem into a black hole.

Endless silence, before she dispelled it.

'How long will you stay in Sana'a?'

An electric shock: her accent had changed! She didn't pronounce the 'q' in the word *setabqa* (will you stay) as a 'g', as people in Sana'a do: *setabga*. She pronounced the word with a clear, fluent Adeni q-sound, an accent she perhaps hadn't used since she left Aden ten years earlier.

'Are you Faten from Saif al-Ariqi's shop?' I asked, stuttering in astonishment.

'Promise me you'll never mention that pervert's name again, or my former life in Aden.'

A whirl of astonishment. I started to stutter. Faced with her, I became a speechless young boy again, as silent as I had been in the blind man's shop, and just as weak. Unable to find something to say, or take the initiative.

Then the words escaped my lips, unconsciously rising up, flying out; I couldn't catch them or put them in order.

'It's not possible, I don't believe it! I have a thousand questions about our silent meetings in the blind man's shop. I don't get it, it's impossible: how did you become a Salafi? You, Suslov's daughter? Why are you going by Ama al-Rahman now?'

'I'm telling you for the last time,' she said curtly, preparing to leave me forever, 'Promise me you won't mention those names again, and that you'll never speak of my former life in Aden.'

'I promise.'

Then a small walkie-talkie in her handbag beeped, like the kind of device the police have. Another mystery: why was she carrying something like that?

Maybe the person on the other end asked her something like, 'Where are you? What street should the march head towards now?' because she responded with a blatant lie. She didn't say she was in the hotel lobby. (And I thought God hated liars!)

'I'm at the back of the march. Turn on Zubairi Street, then Tahrir Street after that.'

Then she left the hotel, heading to the front of a black march that refused to end.

What astonished me most wasn't this black flood (these birds of darkness, shrieking and cawing their extremist slogans), but her, Hawiya.

'I remember how beautiful your hair was back in the blind man's shop,' I said before she left. 'Why do you hide it from people behind that suffocating veil?'

'Ah, I almost forgot to put my niqab back on. What a disaster!'

She put it on, and was eclipsed.

I went straight up to my room, and looked for my eye mask. I only use it rarely, when I'm seeking blind silence. Utter – albeit temporary – death.

I lay down on the bed, incredibly confused. I put on a pitch-black eye mask, and shut my eyes. I descended into thick darkness.

The divine face that had appeared before me for hours in the blind man's shop, the face that filled my night sky in Aden before I travelled to Paris, glowed in front of me now, penetrating the darkness.

It seemed even more fresh, beautiful, and charming than it had been in my childhood.

Since that moment, dear Azazeel, my life has poured down into a bottomless abyss: Hawiya.

Chapter Fifteen

In the months that followed our fateful meeting in the hotel lobby on the periphery of a black march that weighed down on me like a nightmare, I managed to penetrate the hinterlands of her life. From our first meeting, she categorically forbade me from speaking about her past in Aden or her daily life in Sana'a in the guru's palace complex.

Even so, from the moment I met her I'd been transformed into a questioning machine.

'Is it true that someone who kills "infidels" without "martyring" himself, let's say by leaving a bomb in a garbage bin in the metro station, receives the same "reward" as someone who does "martyr" himself?' I once asked Hawiya.

'It's a matter of intent. Anyone who intends to engage in jihad in the name of God will be rewarded, whether he martyrs himself or not.'

'Will he get seventy houris in paradise?'

'That's a fatwa I haven't heard of.'

'What do you think?'

'I don't really have an opinion; it's for the imams to decide. I follow my imams and obey my emirs.'

'Your emirs?'

'Those who lead the jihad of spreading God's word.'

'I love you to death, *qalbi*.'

'I love you more.'

We chatted endlessly, compensating for the long silence of statues in the blind man's shop. We made up for all of our deep, secret, forbidden desires.

The only thing I managed to learn about her were a few secrets I heard from Ibtihal, the wife of a friend who lived in England.

Ibtihal and Hawiya had gone to the same secondary school in Aden. Ibtihal lived in Sana'a after Yemeni unification in 1990, and she ran into her old friend Hawiya at a few women's qat gatherings. These were often in the mansions of important tribal and religious sheikhs' daughters, whose invitations no one turned down.

When Ibtihal and her husband stopped off in France in the autumn of 1998, I invited them out to dinner in Paris. As usual, we dived into conversation about our shared past in Aden in the 1970s and 80s – scientific socialist Aden.

Our daily lives in those days are the greatest puzzle of all. They're truly surreal, and were never really studied in history, so anyone who lived through that period never tires of talking about it. But it's about as much use as chasing mice in a dark room.

Ibtihal told us that her father (one of Suslov's comrades) was assassinated in the War of 1986, and I told her the story of the idiot who refused to shake hands with Najaa because he'd just washed for prayer. Then I asked her about Suslov's daughter, Faten.

'I see her in Sana'a from time to time,' she said.

'I doubt there's anyone else who knows how she fled from Aden to Sana'a before unification.'

'Well, the regime in the South splintered after the war of '86, you know that. The Salafis (especially their leader, Imam al-Hamdani, his networks, and Sheikh Osama bin Laden, whose ancestors were from Hadramout) wanted to seize it quickly. It became their most sacred goal. How could they liberate Afghanistan from the Soviets, when the Soviets occupied their own homeland: South Yemen, the land of "faith and wisdom" east of the Kaaba? Wadi Dawan was the birthplace of a man who emigrated to Saudi Arabia, who began his life there as a porter and ended it as a billionaire, and fathered fifty-two children in between: Mohammed Bin Awad bin Laden. The most famous among them was boy number seventeen, of the famous phrase: "If the Yemeni Socialist Party survives, then I will not". I'm talking about the founder of the jihadi organisation al-Qaeda: Sheikh Osama Bin Laden. His goal in life was to go down in history like his one and only role model: Hassan-i Sabbah. One of Imam al-Hamdani's daughters was a ruthless Salafi activist, a little "Imam-ette", you might say. At women's qat gatherings in Sana'a after the 1986 war, she heard Faten was going through a psychological crisis, due to her parents' neglect and constant fighting. Salafi women had multiplied in Aden after the War of 1986, and were known for their influential and effective discourse. One of them was tasked with meeting Faten. She managed to brainwash and radicalise her by explaining (with dazzling religious simplicity), the reason behind the disaster that was her life: her parents' failure to obey God and his prophet. Signs of God's anger with her parents (and all Communists in

South Yemen) included: the war of January 1986, the scandalous
way both her family and Democratic Yemen fell apart. Then she
offered her an easy way out: just come to the house of a scholar of
the age, God's righteous Sheikh Imam Mohammed al-Hamdani,
the Guide to the Straight Path, at whose prayers the doors to the
seven heavens open wide. The Salafi woman arranged everything
with the imam's daughter. Everything went according to plan:
Faten fled north across the border, even though it was closed, by
going through villages. She arrived at the Imam's family palace
complex in Sana'a, in total secrecy.'

Suslov's daughter had willingly arrived in the home of the
obscurantists' leader, the man who inspired jihadis across the
region. Who would have believed it? Marxism–Leninism had
been reeling from the tragedy of the January 1986 war. But
Salafism dealt the final blow that day.

Ibtihal took a sip of water, the bitterness of the defeated in her
eyes. She lit a cigarette.

*That night, Bin Laden raised a glass of delicious, exquisite,
highly expensive Dawani honey, tantamount to caviar in Yemen,*
I thought bitterly to myself. *Honey found in just one place in the
whole world: Wadi Dawan!*

'She was given an extra week of brainwashing in the imam's
house in the heart of his complex. His staff was highly experienced
in this, and very efficient,' Ibtihal continued. 'It started with
listening to tapes of the imam's lectures over and over. These
were extremely popular in Salafi circles, particularly in Algeria,
in those days. She had to listen to tapes of Sheikh Bin Laden's
lectures too – the man "who gave up his millions for Islam and
the Caliphate State". Imam al-Hamdani considered Bin Laden his

own spiritual father. After this week of "enlightenment", Faten emerged a different person, as if she'd had a brain transplant, living in a state of permanent hypnosis. Of that much I'm sure.'

Hawiya: a veritable abyss.

'Around this time, the imam's staff were working on infiltrating poor communities,' she added. 'Thanks to their proselytising, Salafism was on the rise. News that the daughter of a prominent communist infidel had fled Aden to take refuge in the imam's house in Sana'a was a boon. They said her parents were both abusive – that her father used to rape her, with her mother's knowledge. "He's your father, listen to him," they claimed she'd say. And it was Imam al-Hamdani – a leader among Muslim scholars – who took interest in her himself and saved her. He brought her out of the darkness and into the light, "purified her", and transformed her into a righteous, holy woman. After her successful transformation, his generosity continued. He married her to his favourite son and successor: young Imam Omar, may God be pleased with him!'

Ibtihal let out a long sigh. 'At any rate, she's a different woman now. She changed her name and accent. Practically nobody knows the whole story.'

Thank you, Ibtihal!

Since Hawiya and I had first started seeing each other, I'd noticed the way she spoke about Imam al-Hamdani, and the way her expression changed whenever he came up. I'd become more and more convinced that their relationship wasn't an innocent one. A thousand explanations and scenarios appeared in my mind after I spoke to Ibtihal in France that time. I always came back to these two:

Maybe the sheikh had fallen in love with Hawiya when she arrived at his palace. Like a feral predator, he believed that she was God's gift to him: a willing young girl, given to him by God to use in his war against communism. And fuck his way through jihad, simply put.

Or, perhaps after a week (at most) of religious brainwashing, he successfully had her in his clutches. (Obscurantists had more than ten centuries' worth of experience in such brainwashing after all.) He became her mystical saviour, the one who pulled her life out of the darkness and into the light of truth and faith. A leader she had to obey blindly, because 'what the Sheikh wanted, God wanted.'

I'll never understand how he made her fall in love with him. Not even cognitive science experts could understand it.

But I'm sure that '*What can I do? He won't have it!*' were the words of a slave to her master. Of a prisoner, down to the bone. Of a daughter, raped by her own father. Trained since childhood to fear and obey him absolutely.

Why didn't he marry her himself?

I know he had four wives, and children with each one. Maybe servant girls too: slaves and servants aren't forbidden in Islam, only in international law, and that was quite recent. As a strict Salafi, he despised international regulations that conflicted with the way of life in an Islamic Caliphate as he imagined it: 'our righteous forefathers' legacy, which they entrusted us to guard with our lives,' as he often said.

Even so, it would have been quite easy for him to divorce one of them to marry Hawiya. But he didn't.

Maybe he really did love her, and didn't want her to be another piece of his property like his wives and servants.

Maybe with her, and only her, he could be his true self. Maybe it reminded him of when he was a Don Juan student in Beirut, who liked to comb his hair like Elvis Presley, before he flunked his first year of medical school – twice.

That failure had shaken him to the core and changed his life. He realised that late nights studying, hard work, scientific achievements, civil society, and a pompadour like Elvis Presley's wouldn't get him ahead in life.

He was an influential and eloquent orator, masterful in deceit and brainwashing. Nothing more.

Nothing more.

According to General Sun Tzu's famous sixth century BC treatise, *The Art of War,* a combatant must attack from his points of strength and sacrifice his points of weakness.

In Beirut, al-Hamdani linked up with a Salafi terrorist circle. They admired him and decided he would be the key to penetrating Yemen, the 'land of faith and wisdom'.

He returned to Yemen, and shortly after arriving in Sana'a, requested a teaching position at the College of Sharia and Law – even though he didn't have a university degree.

The dean of the college was a well-qualified, secular-minded professor. He had fled Aden after it was seized by gangs who believed in 'violence for violence'.

At first the dean rejected al-Hamdani's request. Maybe the man had forgotten he was nothing but a weak civilian. That he'd fled from a city of fierce tribal violence, which could swallow him up in minutes.

Before long, the dean gave in. He succumbed to orders from the President of the University of Sana'a, tribal and political pressure, and continuous threats, especially after he noticed the elite's complicit silence and terrible hypocrisy. He realised the imam and the entire elite were just pawns in the state's hands. In a game of special interests, the mafiosi regime could move them however it wanted.

A few months after al-Hamdani was given the job, the dean noticed that this new professor was spending all his time brainwashing the students. He selected them carefully and told them about 'the ungodly West, which teaches children how to have sex in primary school, and wants us (the country of faith and wisdom) to become like them.' He spoke to them about how urgent it was to return to 'the Islamic caliphate state, and the truth,' that it was 'our righteous forefathers' legacy, which they entrusted us to guard with our lives.'

'Which they entrusted us to guard with our lives,' he said slowly, in dulcet tones that intrigued them all. Myself included, dear Azazeel.

(I see a slight angelic smile on my friend's lips.)

With financial support and other means, he recruited them to distribute tapes of his speeches to the masses. They became his own personal militia, who dedicated their lives to memorising and repeating what he said.

'My faith in Imam al-Hamdani is like mother's milk. I'll kill anyone who insults him,' wrote one of his mujahideen once. A whole generation of aspiring 'houri-fuckers' were raised on the imam's books, speeches, and philosophy.

On a day that was much like a day in the late eleventh century when Hassan-i Sabbah seized the fortress of Alamut Castle, the dean of the college summoned him to his office.

'These students are young. They came here to study science, not to be recruited for partisan activity,' the dean told al-Hamdani. 'The things you tell them are harmful, and it's damaging the college's reputation.'

'You have two choices, and five minutes,' responded the Imam.

'Pardon?'

'You can retire and sign over the college administration to me right now. Or I can tell the forty people waiting outside this door that you're a communist infidel. That you want to turn North Yemen into a communist country like the one you came from across the border. And that you want to prevent the word of God from spreading amongst His soldiers in this pure land!'

The dean of the college looked out the window of his office to see forty fanatics at the door, each armed with a *janabi* dagger, waiting to see how the meeting would end.

Five minutes later, he left his office through a side door. Just a week after that, he fled to a country in the Gulf with his family, where he lived for the rest of his life.

The imam imposed an obscurantist curriculum for all students in all schools across the Yemen Arab Republic. But he wasn't satisfied, not with this or with being Dean of the College of Sharia. His failure in the college of Medicine in Beirut, and the complex he developed as a result, were going to stay with him for the rest of his life.

He had to hear people call him 'a modern Avicenna' to loosen the grip of his deep insecurities even slightly.

He became a quack, inventing 'Quranic miracle drugs' to treat diseases that modern medicine couldn't, from AIDS to cancer.

The Ministry of Health refused to give this charlatan a medical licence, just as any ministry on Earth would. They couldn't approve his treatments because – quite simply – there was nothing medical about them.

So in order to obtain a license, he resorted to calling them infidels, as usual.

He telephoned the official at the Ministry who was responsible for licences, and calmly told him, 'You have fifteen minutes to send me the licence, or I'll tell everyone you're an infidel, who doesn't believe in Prophetic medicine, divine miracles in the Quran, or the word of God!'

The imam's media team went on and on about this 'modern Avicenna' and his Quranic miracle drugs, which were more effective than modern medicine.

And hospitals in countries bordering Yemen went on and on about his patients ('his drugged sacrificial lambs,' as the staff called them), who arrived on their doorstep half-dead.

An old friend of his from Beirut recently posted an old picture of him on Facebook. He is the spitting image of Elvis Presley. Everyone else was shocked, but I really like it.

He looks like a movie star, as if he could have played Abdel Halim Hafez's role in *Dad Over the Tree*. Or maybe Eli Wallach's role in *The Good, the Bad, and the Ugly*, since he didn't have an ounce of the Dark Nightingale's kind countenance.

Today, pictures of the 'guru' of the 'land of faith and wisdom,' show a man with skin like leather; a maniacal artificial smile; a dazed, meditative gaze that could penetrate the six heavens; a henna-dyed beard; wrinkles the years have carved on his skin; and a dark *zebiba* prayer mark across his forehead (instead of a *foosha,* the pompadour of his Beirut youth); all under an enormous pile of Gaddafi-esque overcoats, colourful scarves, and heavy religious turbans.

Although he married Hawiya to his son, his relationship with her continued in secret. To me, he's filthy, gross, vile beyond compare. Maybe he hated his son more than I can imagine.

His son truly was his heir. I know a lot about him. Hawiya only married him to obey his father, for no other reason. But she's hated him fiercely from the first day they met.

Before being alone with her on their wedding night, he first went to pray two *rakaat.* But he returned giving off a nasty stench she hasn't forgotten to this day. He was drunk, very drunk. In truth, he returned to rape her. 'A violent, crazed monster,' she said. He forced himself inside her, and was thrilled when she bled. Her screams from that moment still echo in her ears, and likely won't fade for as long as she lives.

Her hatred hadn't let up since that dark, brutal night. She loathed him, 'fiercely and vehemently,' as she often said darkly.

Hawiya came to see his daily drunkenness as a blessing, because for those hours she was completely free. She usually came back at night, when he was dead to the world. She knew he would stay that way until prayer time. Her life continued, as did her affair with his father the tyrant, a man she had submitted to unconsciously, with a mysterious, metaphysical, magnetic passion.

When I returned to Paris, Sheikh Mohamed al-Hamdani became a recurring nightmare, and my greatest obsession. I didn't know how to free Hawiya (and myself) from his clutches.

Whenever I thought of his name (which was most of the time), I could feel my arteries suddenly constrict right through

to the capillaries, and my blood pressure rise. My spine would
freeze and my brain would boil like an ulcer about to burst.

Meanwhile, I daydreamed: I would bring her to live with
me, here in Paris. We would travel the world together, from
Sydney to Santiago, and she wouldn't wear a niqab or a veil, or
even long sleeves. She'd wear light, flowing dresses and look
so radiant. Her beauty, grace, and soft skin would be exposed
to the world, and she could wander freely through the streets
without a care.

I was sure the day would come when she would leave that
quagmire and come to live with me. It would be soon; it was
inevitable.

In anticipation, I bought her a red dress with sleeves that just
came down to the elbows. It was made of pure silk brocade, and
rather expensive. I knew it would fit her, clinging sexily to her
graceful body.

When I imagined her in Paris, it was only ever in that dress.
I touched it every day, touching her in it. It was just as soft as her
own smooth skin.

Then I bought a sapphire-coloured muslin dress, embroidered
with velvet flowers of the same shade. I set it aside for cultural
venues and evenings in classy restaurants.

I described these two dresses to her during one of our
love-ins, and told her they were waiting for her in Paris.
I told her about my dreams where she flitted across the seven
seas, from the most beautiful beaches and islands to the finest
restaurants.

She smiled, and didn't say no. (Salafis don't like the word
'No'; they're advised not to use it except when saying *There is*

no god but God . . .) She didn't make the slightest tangible effort towards that dream, though, or evince a convincing desire for us to reunite in Paris.

Months passed, then years, and we drew no closer to that fantasy. For me, rescuing her became an urgent, even revolutionary quest. This incredible beauty was the same woman who supplied obscurantists with female proselytisers, and filled the streets of Sana'a with birds of darkness during million-woman marches. She would be the best deposit in my account I could show the Angel of Revolutions on Judgment Day.

Yemen entered a spiral of political conflict in 2006, and things have worsened since 2009. The country has been threatening to descend into a level of chaos, war, and destruction from which it wouldn't emerge. The Southern Movement called for South Yemen to secede (it rejected the union of North and South Yemen, and felt the South had been occupied by the North since the 1994 Yemeni Civil War). There were endless wars between the regime and the Houthis in Saada. And practically the whole country staunchly rejected the regime.

My secret, noble relationship with Hawiya continued. The fiery, rejuvenating joy of our love-ins didn't diminish. But my destined reunion abroad with this beautiful woman no longer seemed imminent.

I brought her lots of gifts from Paris in the hope it would somehow connect her to the city, subconsciously. I tried to steer things my way: I spent hours describing cities in the West, their cultural traditions and their freedom, the trips and discoveries that lay ahead for us there.

She always daydreamed while listening to me, with a childlike smile. Then she'd suddenly interrupt, like someone exorcising a demon who'd tried to sneak into his brain as he was praying.

Then she'd make me 'enter her', as she liked to say, so we could continue the orchestra of our paradise sessions, which she preferred to my stories.

She would close her eyes as I drowned in her. Maybe she was travelling far away, to the distant beaches and islands it was pointless describing to her.

When the Yemeni revolution began, on 11 February 2011, I came very close to realising that dream. Or perhaps I went much further away from it. I don't know.

Chapter Sixteen

Post on my Facebook wall:

As Zine El Abidine Ben Ali was fleeing Tunisia on his plane, searching for a country to take him in, I was writing my first article: 'The Time Has Come for Yemen's Tyrant to Depart'. The moment I finished it, I sent it to a long list of editors and contacts.

Not a single Arab newspaper agreed to publish it. It was ahead of its time.

It was rejected by print newspapers for days, until an online newspaper agreed to publish it, at the end of January 2011. I'll always be thankful to the editor: S.S.

Post on my Facebook wall:

On the eve of 11 February I sat frozen in my chair at the office. I followed Omar Suleiman's speech on my computer screen, practically paralysed. Everyone was waiting for him to read Mubarak's resignation speech. Instead, he read a speech that said the complete opposite; no one could make any sense of it.

Honestly, I was paralysed. (I realised then how someone could die isolated and alone in their home, with neither a comrade nor a friend. How one's putrefying body could be discovered only after days, weeks, or longer.)

After his speech, the internet broadcast out of Egypt was interrupted. Abroad, there was universal despair.

A prominent Egypt expert wrote something on Facebook that really needled me: 'Mubarak won't leave! People are making a lot of noise for nothing.'

Shocking!

I couldn't leave my office chair, or at least I didn't want to. Actual paralysis, albeit benign. I might have nodded off for a few hours before dawn. I stayed there, willingly paralysed, until the following afternoon. On February 11, Omar Suleiman towered stiffly on screen in his smart blue suit. He read a brief statement, just four lines long, in perfect classical Arabic: Mubarak's resignation.

The paralysed man dances, leaps, flies.

I called every friend in the universe to share my joy.

Post on my Facebook wall:

Oh, the things Gaddafi has cost me:

When the news of Misrata's Tripoli Street being bombed came through I followed it in horror. I watched videos on my iPhone whilst driving. I ran red lights and other traffic signs. As a result: I got ten points on my driver's licence, out of the twelve it takes before they revoke it. All thanks to Tripoli Street!

That's not all. I lost my backpack, the one that had practically become part of me over the decades. (I'd carried a backpack since my first year in university. It was the first present my wife had given me, along with a fountain pen. From that day on, I never went anywhere without it).

I lost it in Paris, along with all the precious documents and belongings it held. I'd been out walking and had stopped on a quiet street corner, to follow breaking news about Tripoli Street on my iPhone.

I stood there for half an hour, maybe, and got so worked up that I went on my way without picking up the backpack like I usually always did without a second thought. It was as if I'd left a part of my body sitting there on the ground.

I returned to the same spot three hours later to look for it. Without luck. Oh, the things Misrata has cost me!

I wanted to withdraw three hundred euros from a cashpoint on the street before going to buy *Le Monde*, the evening newspaper, and catch up on what had been happening on Tripoli Street. I was in such a hurry that I put my card in the cash point, took it out again, and rushed off towards the shop without taking the money that came out after I'd withdrawn my card.

I didn't realise what I'd done until I tried to pay for the newspaper: my pocket had nothing in it except for the bankcard!

If I meet Gaddafi on Judgment Day my list of what he owes me will be long.

It includes two plane tickets: I lost them thanks to his madness and brutality, and because he turned a peaceful uprising into a military conflict.

The first ticket was during the bombing of Misrata. I was on my way to a conference in Poland. For more than twenty years I'd taken the metro from the Gare du Nord in Paris to the Charles de Gaulle Airport at least twice a month. But this time I took it in the opposite direction, towards Orly Airport.

I missed the flight and lost my hotel booking because I was sitting on the metro, absorbed in news of Misrata, not paying attention to the stations. I knew them by heart, and didn't realise I was passing them in the opposite direction.

I lost the second ticket when the Libyan revolution descended into military conflict. I was in Beauvais-Tillé Airport on my way to Sardinia. I stayed in a café at the airport too long because I was watching the news and discussing Gaddafi and how horrible he was with a wonderful woman next to me. I didn't realise the gate had closed.

Post on my Facebook wall:

The best parts of the Yemeni revolution took place in 'Freedom Square' in Taiz: an incredible commune with engaging artistic and cultural activities. It ushered in an amazing revolution, it seemed.

Then came wave after wave of pain in Aden. The Southern Movement (and the Southern Spring) preceded the Arab Spring by three years. They had been a bone in the regime's throat since 2009.

The regime struck Aden with a horrifying viciousness, seeped in loathing.

Dozens of martyrs fell in Aden, from the first days of the revolution. I felt like I was with them in every hour, every moment.

I know this city's every pain; her blood has been shed since the 1994 Yemeni Civil War. This once charming, cosmopolitan city has become a hotbed of plundering tribes, and a playground for their malice. It was only then that I fully realised the extent of the regime's madness and brutality. Its fixation on extinguishing a revolution that had been waiting to burst into flame since 2009.

'Before Bouazizi, our saint, steeled his nerves to liberate us and let us live, I'd long lost all hope.' (I have to remind myself not to roll my eyes while rereading what I wrote that day.) I didn't just hope to see 'the sunset of capitalism and the dawn of socialism and equality' (I, who loved sunsets). I also hoped to see the sunset of Arab tyrants and their eternal, obscurantist dictatorships. Or even the sunset of one single tyrant.

I nearly lost all hope that Hawiya would leave the swamp that was her life in the Imam's palace complex to travel the world with me as I wanted her to.

I longed fiercely to hold her in those days; I hadn't seen her since the previous summer. We hadn't been apart this long since our first rehearsal for paradise. Because of some professional responsibilities I couldn't avoid, I couldn't go to Sana'a before March 11. In other words: precisely one month after Mubarak fell, and the Yemeni revolution began.

A gust of cherished memories fluttered up to the roof of my mind: I'd put Najaa on my shoulders during le Fête de l'Humanité, protest marches, and artistic performances in France and abroad, so many times. Just like this young man was doing for his girlfriend.

Najaa was gone, and I would never again find someone to sit on my shoulders and tell every dictator in the Blue Planet Archipelago: *irhal!*

She was gone, and had left me alone, dispossessed, no faith left in the world. I lived down in the cellar, in a dubious, deluded love I shared with a *tabeen*, my brother-husband. I was poking a sleeping dragon, calmly waiting to die.

She was gone, a victim to terrorist cells that thrived in these rotten Arab dictatorships. But the Tunisian revolution said to them: *irhal!*

After Tunisia, I lived through Egypt's revolution and the glories of Tahrir Square, minute by minute.

The commune of Tahrir Square was unmistakable – it was everything we'd dreamt of, a new brand of revolution. No vanguard party, no Bolsheviks, no Mensheviks. Just an epic, timeless square, and an ingenious, modern weapon: the internet.

Hope blossomed, brighter and brighter, once Libya joined the revolutionary ranks too. I was on the train when Gaddafi delivered his *Zenga Zenga* speech. I watched it on my iPad, shaking. I couldn't believe my eyes, watching the 'King of Kings' of Africa so pathetic and exposed. The more he puffed himself up, the more broken down he appeared. I pitied him, I really did.

Despite this, he managed to turn the revolution into an armed conflict. He began a heavy aerial assault on the people.

As I followed the military bombing campaign on Tripoli Street in Misrata, my joys ended. I shook in fear every day, as if I lived there with my children and grandchildren.

Everything changed: revolution shifted towards madness and war.

Even so, my ears were constantly pricked for the heartbeat of Yemen's revolution.

My desire to hold Hawiya grew.

I longed for love-ins and rehearsals for paradise in this new era: the early days of the revolution.

March 11, 2011:

Early in the morning, my plane landed in the capital of Yemen's revolutionary spring: Sana'a.

Frightening conditions, and anxiety from the moment we landed. I argued over everything with the taxi driver who took me from the airport to the flat.

'Why did you come at a time like this? Are you mad?'

'Are you joking? I should have been here a month ago! I've been waiting for an eternity, I wish I could have got a load of this stunner from day one!'

'Who's the lucky lady?'

'Lady? I'm talking about the revolution!'

'What revolution?'

'The Yemeni revolution!'

'The Yemeni revolution, hah! Good luck...'

I said nothing.

'It sounded like you were talking about a woman,' he finally grumbled, disentangling the confusion I'd made of his questions.

Despite his skepticism, I really did feel I could see something like a revolution unfolding, something like hope blooming. Pictures of the dictator had been torn off walls, new chants sprang up here and there, calls for others to join in, I overheard rebellious conversations in the airport and while crossing the city. Sana'a was divided between two powers:

The first camp held the regime and the military. Their thugs had quickly pitched their tents in Tahrir Square, near Tahrir Street in old Sana'a. They were afraid the revolutionaries would occupy it and turn it into an echo of Cairo's Tahrir Square, which had toppled Mubarak. (Yemen's Tahrir Square had borrowed its name from Egypt's at the start of the North Yemen Civil War in 1962, when the revolutionary republicans staged a coup d'état).

The second camp held the revolutionaries and the protesters. They had massed in the streets and the square by the university as an alternative to Tahrir Square, and renamed it 'Change Square'.

Thus, Sana'a mirrored two contrasting rhymed lines from a stanza of classical Arabic *amoudi* poetry. The first line ended with the word *liberation*. The second line ended with *transformation*.

Some might say the first line should have ended with *repudiation* (because all religious extremists intent on repudiating nonbelievers belonged to the first camp). And that the second should have ended with *detonation* (because all criminals and bombing experts belonged to the second camp).

Transformation, repudiation, liberation, detonation.

But now, Sana'a snapped every hackneyed rhyme in two. The world watched in surprise;

Indifference;

Vague awareness;

And then surprise, mixed with a bit of awe.

It was clear as I was crossing Sana'a towards my flat.

Less than three months after Bouazizi passed away, the walls of fear in people's minds had truly fallen. It was obvious.

I remembered Sartre's words: *Once liberty has exploded in the soul of a man, the Gods can do nothing against him.*

The dream expanded in my mind, stretching and extending out in every direction.

I arrived at the flat out of breath. I wanted to wash, but the water refused to come out of the tap. Eventually a few cold drops laboriously made their way out. I was eager to go to Change Square, on the edge of Sana'a University campus (the centre of Yemen's revolutionary commune), to join the crowds for the Friday of Anger. I'd been following the news on Al Jazeera while waiting at the parched tap.

Revolutionary energy coursed through me like a fever. I was finally experiencing the historical moment I'd been awaiting since I was born, or even before that. I might not experience the sunset of capitalism in my life, as Najaa and I had often dreamed. But at least I would experience the sunset of dictatorship and the dawn of a new Arab world, first hand!

I arrived at Change Square just before Friday prayers, to an incredible revolutionary atmosphere, one I couldn't have even imagined. Protesters' tents were everywhere. All the revolutionaries were writing their dreams on pieces of paper and sticking them to their tents or taping them to their backs.

A tapestry of dreams. I wish I'd collected them all in a book, instead of just memorising a few. I took pictures with my phone, though. Here's what one young woman from the countryside wrote, just how I saw it on her tent:

'My dream: a Toyota Hilux, big enough to fit a ton of stuff. I'll load it up with the best qat from Anss and drive all the way from al-Janad to Tihama, then on to Aden. I'll pick up hitchhikers, only let them pitch in for petrol, oil, and stuff, and listen to their stories on the way down South. I dream of marrying Walid. He's a mamma's boy, tied to his mother's apron, but he listens to his father and I know he'll follow in his footsteps. I dream of owning a laptop bag with two sections: one for a laptop, and another for a sweet Russian machine gun. I'll look for a widow to cover my job at the media office, and give her half my salary in return. With the other half (three million rial) I'll set up a charitable foundation, and I'll take one month's worth of its profits a year, so I can go on Haj with my mother and father. Then by 2015 I'll publish my first novel: *The Girl from Az'zal.*'

I often reread this innocent dream, which grew from the bedrock of a sweet young country girl's mind. I remember catching her name – Salma – while passing her tent and her group of friends.

An outpouring of sincerity. Grace of spirit. I knelt before their tent; I walked past on tiptoe.

Intimate conversations, revolutionary music, protest chants here and there, discussion circles, prayers, religious speeches . . .

I was reminded of le Fête de l'Humanité, the yearly pilgrimage Najaa and I made. It was our eternal passion (we, who wished life would be an endless fête de l'humanité, as big as the whole world). Compared to Change Square, it seemed like another world.

Silent tears: it was the first time I'd seen something in Sana'a that reminded me of Najaa.

Where is she now, dear Smiter of Souls?

What did you do with her pure spirit, you heartless angel? Where in the Valley of Tears does her spirit soar now? Will I meet her again? Believe it or not, dear Ender of Delights and Breaker of Desires: every so often, I still dream that she's on her way home from the Gibert-Joseph bookstore, carrying a bag filled with books and a bundle of pencils.

I wish I could walk through Change Square with her today, and stand up to the tribes.

I was walking through a real live revolutionary commune. I spent time in tents where people upheld secular slogans, tents of university staff, tents of the Yemeni Socialist party. My heart swelled with hope and joy.

I felt the same metaphysical bliss that Najaa and I had been filled with when we lost ourselves in massive concerts celebrating life, hope and revolution: that old feeling was welling up inside me again now.

I rarely went near tents of tribesmen, Salafis, the Muslim Brotherhood, or Houthis (followers of Imam Al al-Batnein: the descendants of Hassan and Hussein).

In other words: I rarely went near most of the tents there.

People of all kinds mixed in the Square: from conservative Salafis (who formed the vast majority), to the odd secularist. From the vast number of tribesmen to experienced civil society activists scattered here and there. From the downtrodden illiterate, or semi-literate folk to the enlightened and educated. From the impoverished lumpenproletariat (as we used to call them in revolutionary communist Aden) with dirt under his fingernails, to the well-dressed intellectual.

What a hodgepodge! *Charabia*, as they say in imported French. *Aseed,* in Yemeni.

I was certain that the 'seven honourable sons' who had liked most of my Facebook posts were there too, somewhere in the square. Maybe I'd even seen them.

If they hadn't used fake names and profile pictures on Facebook (just like I did), we would have been able to recognise each other. We could have embraced each other as friends, or toasted our first meeting in person: with a glass of mango juice, nothing stronger.

There was no beer in the Square, obviously. (The factory in Aden had been shut down by obscurantists during the 1994 Yemeni Civil War, to benefit the alcohol smugglers: senior members of the regime and army.) The most delicious taste to linger in my memory was still Sirah Beer.

Just like any normal week: in the heart of the square, people got ready for Friday prayer, right after a revolutionary religious sermon.

The call to prayer, and then the prayers themselves, shook the square.

As someone who knew the danger of taking religion out of the mosque and into the street I was worried by religion's presence in the revolution. Despite that, my heart trembled with joyous, astonished hope.

I'd made a clean break with religion at fourteen, when I fell in love at first sight with Politzer's hundredth degree. Now I asked myself: why not join Friday prayer?

I would pray with all my heart for the revolution to be victorious. For the ruling family to fall, and Yemen to make a new start.

I would ask God to let Hawiya *leave*, just like was being demanded of all these Arab dictators. To let her come with me into this vast world, so we could live in Aden by the sea (on my eponymous Imran Island). Or even in Imran, close to Sana'a, this nasty city I'd somehow fallen in love with, away from Hawiya's vile guru: my 'brother husband', Imam al-Hamdani, and his palace complex.

Where was he?

Imam al-Hamdani – a man the regime used to consider its own flesh and blood – was now one of the President's most major opponents. He and his son, Imam Omar, had fled to a neighbouring country for fear of being attacked by the regime's security forces. His sermons had stirred up the faithful public, and mobilised them against the regime.

Deep in my heart, my hopes redoubled. Hawiya's tormentor had fled; she was now far from him and his son, her detestable husband. I just needed to take advantage of this opportunity, to save her from them once and for all. I might not have another chance.

Hope and contradictions, fused: my arch rival was one of the most important 'ideologues' of the revolution (his revolution and my revolution, fused). He was an important figurehead and leader, and an inspiration for many revolutionaries.

Can you understand this maddening equation, dear Reaper, or even begin to solve it?

As for me, I couldn't understand a thing. My brain's fuses blew every time I tried.

Was this a revolution or a trap?

Was it better to have leukaemia (the current regime) or brain cancer (a Salafi regime)? The plague or cholera?

The worst part: at the vanguard of this revolution was a woman, one of its leaders and central figures. Just like Joan of Arc, dear Angel of the Dead, believe it or not.

The tent she shared with several proselytiser friends was one of the first to be pitched in the square. They slept there day and night. She led revolutionary protest chants, and the young and old alike chanted after her. A Yemeni Joan of Arc. ('The Nutter' as one of the seven honourable sons called her in a Facebook post, without realising how his insult stung me.)

She emerged from her tent every morning right after breakfast, like a coach for a team of young revolutionaries. Everyone bowed down before her steadfast opposition to the regime. She challenged it with a fearlessness that was not without a certain extremism.

They called her a heroine, and 'a woman worth a thousand men'.

In a fresh voice, this Yemeni Joan of Arc chanted (just as al-Hassani did when we were kids):

'*Each time another martyr falls*'

And instantly, fanatics responded (just as we responded to al-Hassani):

'*All revolutionaries gain resolve!*'

Who was she?

A woman who seemed younger than her age. She was thirty-three, just six years younger than me. A religious proselytiser who had taken off her niqab the moment the revolution broke out, and revealed her gorgeous face to the world. Everyone bowed down when they saw her.

Ever since the revolution had begun, I had been spending half my time in Paris following updates about her on Facebook, and tracking her interviews with television stations and newspapers from around the world.

That was how, slowly but surely, my silent interlocutor from the blind man's shop was ringing in a new era of revolution across the world.

But why did she take off her niqab? She'd never expressed the slightest desire to do so before.

Was it an auspicious effect of the revolution? Proof of real change blossoming in the consciousness of the woman I loved? A glimmer of hope?

Or had someone in the party forced her to become the international female face of the revolution? Was there an unwritten rule somewhere that foreign journalists and Gulf television channels should clamour to photograph and interview her?

Would I see her in the square? Would she come to my flat a few hours later, after I'd left Change Square and gone home to await our rehearsals for paradise, as I always did? I longed for them even more fiercely now, like never before.

I could barely imagine how incredible our love-ins in the throes of the revolution were going to be. Hawiya had liberated herself from her niqab, Imam al-Hamdani, and her husband, Imam Omar. As leaders of the opposition, they had fled the President's vengeance and gone abroad.

The hour of Friday prayer approached. Everyone, without exception, headed towards an open space in the heart of Change Square.

Why shouldn't I pray like everyone else?

I didn't hesitate! I dived into the crowds of worshippers with enthusiasm, and a bit of humility. (I'd completely forgotten you have to do ablution before prayer.)

I knelt in the last row so I could hear the sermon. After a moment, I realised this 'revolutionary' preacher was a well-known fiqh scholar who opposed the ban on child marriage: Sheikh Abdul Rahman. Imam Omar Mohamed al-Hamdani's unfailing friend through thick and thin was here in the flesh.

I twitched.

Praying behind a criminal who thought it was fine to fuck children was definitely against my beliefs.

Suddenly I asked myself: what was I doing here? Had listening to this disaster of a man speak made me go mad? Had I no shame, listening to a criminal?

A few minutes later: choking anxiety. A desire to leave the square, close the book of 'revolution', and not look back.

His speech: antediluvian, unscientific notions of a supposed history I didn't recognise at all. Hypnotism, brainwashing.

(I notice the Snatcher of Souls looks displeased with a revolution that ushers in the most despicable obscurantists. I hear a sigh of regret. I try to soften the blow of what I'm telling my friend, who hates charlatans' masks and hypocrisy even more than I do.)

I took refuge from Sheikh Abdul Rahman's racket in my memories, dear Breaker of Desires:

I remembered praying in the mosque in Aden as a boy, before Politzer's 'hundredth degree' put me in a leg lock at age fourteen.

I loved the fans (which relieved the scorching heat and thick humidity), and their sweet simplicity. Bright red iced Vimto and sweets given to everyone after night prayer in the mosque. (Memorial services were called 'lessons', and followed by people reciting the Quran to bless the soul of the departed. I was always overcome with emotion whilst listening to that orchestra of murmurs under the mosque's glaring neon lights and through the roar of the electric fans.)

So began praying on the Friday of Anger. I noticed, happily, that I still remembered the rituals of prayer: the words, intonation, motions.

Just before the end, as everyone was kneeling and silently mouthing the *tashahhud,* a small child who had come to pray with his father stood up. In the middle of the worshippers deep in prayer, he arose and chanted: '*The people want to bring down the regime!*' His words sent untold energies coursing through me. (I used to repeat these words to myself while walking in Paris or down the corridors at home: individual 'million man marches' like those in Egypt and Yemen every Friday.)

I could barely suppress my laughter, even in the middle of prayer. This child was standing and reciting his favourite verse to himself, while everyone else knelt in worship!

What a potent symbol: a child standing among kneeling adults, I said to myself. Revolutionary 'propaganda and self-incitement' like that always lifted my spirits.

To each his own hypnosis, dear Destroyer of Delights.

As soon as prayer ended, other people like me stood up to chant after the boy: *The people want to bring down the regime!* The leaders of the Organising Committee weren't pleased. They'd been chanting this phrase less frequently, and a bit sourly when they did. They'd abandoned it in favour of other, more religious chants.

I noticed: they were actually annoyed by those two words, *the people want*. It vexed them. Because only the ruler, the king, the one in power, could *want*. The people were only there only to obey the king, sheikh, ruler, or Organising Committee.

If the people truly *did* want, it was the beginning of the end.

Thus, the central question (and I didn't know the answer to it): were the people truly able *to want*?

Most worshippers followed the preacher's additional supplications and praise to God after the group prayer ended, unhappy with our rebellious group's deviance. We started to circle the square, chanting *the people want to bring down the regime* after this little maestro, who was conducting us from his father's shoulders.

The orthodox protesters would only start marching when the Organising Committee announced Friday's 'million man march' through the 'liberated' streets of divided Sana'a.

Abdel Rahman's prayers ended with the words, 'God – destroy the infidels.' For a moment, I felt like I was suffocating. He was lighting the way for people like those who put explosives in a rubbish bin in the Saint-Michel metro!

God, what was I doing here? What was I doing here?

While waiting to join the larger march, I chanted along with our rebellious little group. As brazen as my vocal chords could be, as mellifluously as I could muster, I recited my most sacred verse: *The people want to bring down the regime!* I poured tons of dormant energy into these words, with unbounded happiness.

I wanted to shout that phrase until I collapsed, unconscious, in the middle of Change Square. I wanted to be swallowed whole by the square, down into its belly. I needed eruptions, uprisings, madness!

We marched between tents and through side streets, on the periphery of the much larger, official march. Our little, joyful, rebellious crowd was ready to join in.

As we approached a tent showing a film about women's role in the Yemeni revolution, I split off from the march. The film was going to be screened in an international film festival, and I was sure it would focus on a star of the revolution: Hawiya.

I went into the tent, and sat down with the people crammed inside it.

On the right side sat a few women, dressed in black, while the left side was packed with men, most of them from neighbouring tribes. Between the two sides was a distance that was not to be crossed.

The strangest thing was that according to the Organising Committee, husbands had to sit on the men's side of the tent, apart from their wives.

God, was this the revolution that was going to lead us onwards to Kandahar?

I left the tent. I couldn't stand these obscurantist customs. Besides, I was sure I could find the film on YouTube, and see Hawiya fill the screen, without a niqab.

A shy old man with a swollen face, a round paunch, and the sharp sense of humour people from Dhamar are known for was sitting by the tent opposite. He noticed me grumbling. He stared into the masses with insightful eyes, and the levity of someone collecting sights and memories as raw materials for jokes and banter when he returned to Dhamar.

'What's the matter *ya Haj*,' he asked me. 'Didn't you like the film?'

'It hasn't started yet. But to be honest, I don't like how the tent's organisers are running it. They say they're revolutionaries, but they've separated men and women, even husbands and wives.'

'*Ya ibni*, you see everyone here in the square? They all take after their fathers, who were Republicans in the morning and Monarchists in the evening.'

(That is: during the North Yemen Civil War, they first supported the revolutionary republicans, who staged a coup to dethrone the newly crowned Imam. Then, after the Imam had fled to the Saudi border and rallied support there, they supported him during the decisive siege of Sana'a in 1967.)

'Don't believe these Republarchists for a minute!' the man continued. 'They don't want change. They're the biggest hypocrites in the world, just like their fathers and grandfathers before them. Don't believe them for a minute!' He paused a moment, and then added, 'But I'm optimistic – the revolution will succeed.'

I smiled and breathed a sigh of relief. I wanted to kiss his head to thank him for the glad tidings, but then I realised they contradicted what he'd just said.

'Don't buy it so fast,' he added. 'Didn't you notice my optimism's just as hypocritical?'

A yellow smile.

His words stuck in my mind. As the days went by, I thought about them often.

I didn't see that shrewd man from Dhamar again. He passed through my life the way Hitchcock appears in a few of his own films: for mere seconds.

He passed through it like the Prophet Khidr. (According to the Surah of the Cave in the Quran, Khidr was the one who taught Prophet Moses the true nature of things, beyond a simplistic, superficial understanding.)

I called him: Khidr from Dhamar.

I was reluctant to go to Hawiya's tent. From posts about the revolution on Facebook, I knew it was in the heart of the square.

In several videos on YouTube, I'd seen that she was always surrounded by a troop of revolutionary youth in training. Hawiya and her female proselytiser friends were in charge of preparing for the 'glorious march', as they called it. It would be the decisive day: an attack on the presidential palace, to the rhythm of the chant: *Each time another martyr falls, all revolutionaries gain resolve!*

Dear Reaper, can you explain the relationship between this violent revolution and her childhood (which she spent in the throes of an historic war between Suslov and Fairuz)?

I didn't dare go near her tent, the most sacred part of the square, even though I knew she wasn't there. She was out in the square, leading a march that roared through the liberated areas of Sana'a on the Friday of Anger.

But for the past twelve years, we'd never met face to face, other than in my flat. The account balance of our meetings, dear Reaper, was as follows:

Once at my sister Samia's. Once in the hotel lobby (birds of darkness were flocking past us, chanting an extraordinarily secular slogan: *Sharia permits four wives*). And over three hundred rehearsals for paradise.

Since we'd first met in my sister's house, we'd known nothing aside from life inside a flat with the shutters closed tight. We'd never gone out on the balcony, or into the street. We'd never walked under the sun together, on the beach or in the mountains. We'd never sat in a café, a square, or on the roof of a building. We'd never lounged on a desert dune or under the moon. We'd never shared an umbrella in the rain. We did nothing but fuck like mice in a dark cellar.

There was no way of knowing how shocked I would be (and how shocked she would be, too) if I were to see Hawiya in front of me in the square, or if I ran into her on the street. Even for me, who spent half my Paris nights imagining us traveling the world together.

On the other side of the square, near the official platform, I saw two revolutionaries getting married. My heart danced with joy.

Joy and wonder beat in my chest as I approached the celebration.

There I was, about to attend my first ever wedding in Yemen, a revolutionary wedding! This happiness would surely last forever.

I imagined Hawiya and myself sitting where the bride and groom were, flanked by men and women in two separate sections.

Could I – someone who believed in enlightenment and equality between men and women – agree to get married like that?

Why not? What harm was there in watering down the wine (or the milk, as is perhaps more fitting here).

The commotion of the wedding procession and women's ululations washed over me. Sure, I'd gladly water down the milk in exchange for the sounds of this jubilation. Joy pierced my heart like an arrow.

I was in a good mood until I heard several women objecting to the celebration. Some of the 'revolutionary' proselytisers shouted, 'A woman's voice is sinful!' and 'Photography is prohibited, on the Organising Committee's orders!'

A member of the Organising Committee violently ripped a camera away from a revolutionary woman who didn't obey her.

Struggle, kicking.

'Damn the revolution,' I said to myself angrily.

Was the revolution advancing, or retreating to Kandahar?

I changed my mind. I'd never agree to marry Hawiya the way the Organising Committee and Salafi proselytisers would want.

I remembered my conversation with Khidr from Dhamar from a few minutes earlier. How insightful he'd been! It was almost four thirty in the afternoon.

I rushed to find a taxi that would take me back to my flat. For all I knew, maybe Hawiya would go there like she used to before the revolution?

The same eternal ritual: from my window, I surreptitiously watched my neighbour who looked like Yitzhak Shamir. He still hadn't emerged for his trip around the world.

Was he worried about snipers? Afraid of the unknown? Had he passed away?

No, he was still alive. From my window, I could just make him out, moving around the living room. Hesitating. Wanting to venture out. But not leaving the house.

A suffocating certainty settled over me: if he didn't go out, Hawiya wouldn't arrive.

I waited for her with the same old fierce distress. Watching him, losing hope she would come today. My new-old lover. A rising star.

I lost all hope: everything in the city had changed since my last trip. My neighbour didn't even leave his house to circumnavigate the world anymore.

Then, just before six thirty, when silence and fear had burrowed their way into the city, and everything was bathed in darkness, a bus stopped near my building. A girl in a dusty old veil and niqab stepped off. Anyone who saw her would have pitied how poor she was.

It wasn't Hawiya. Although she did look quite similar. She had the same slight, elegant stature.

I would have lost all hope forever, if, just a few minutes later, I hadn't heard a familiar knock on the door.

The girl facing me when I opened the door was wearing a different veil, this one new and chic. But she had the same niqab, and the same scent that turned me on all over again.

The door opened.

The whole of Change Square arrived in my flat.

Chapter Seventeen

Our love-ins after the revolution had broken out differed from those before it. Not just because they united two people with one goal: bringing down the most miserable, corrupt regime Yemen had ever known. (Hawiya and I both trembled with the same revolutionary dream.) The revolution unleashed boundless new energies within us, and we realised, finally, that life had a purpose we had long waited to discover.

Our love-ins after the revolution had a different, unique sensuality to them, one I can hardly describe.

Sex was different, as if we were coming together for the first time. Joined bodies, tears.

'I missed you like I've never missed you before, *wahji*,' I told her.

'I missed you more *habibi*. You were gone so long this time.'

'I was with you in every moment, *qalbi*.'

'And I was with you, always, forever, *hayati*. My nerves were about to explode, I've been so anxious to see you!'

(I loved her, down to her nervous system.)

I quickly noticed there was a small wad of qat leaves in her mouth. She'd never shown up chewing qat before. She knew I couldn't stand seeing it in anyone's cheek, least of all a woman's.

Before the revolution, she used to bring qat to our love-ins every so often. She'd pluck off a couple of leaves in the hours after we made love, rubbing them coquettishly as we chatted in utter contentment. I'd never seen that telltale bulge of qat in her cheek, though.

This time she appeared with her cheek filled with the substance, and I was taken aback. (Even so, she was at the height of her beauty. Her eyes were carefully rimmed with kohl. She had on heavy makeup, as if we weren't in the midst of a revolution, and as if she weren't its star, the person Arab media (particularly Gulf and Saudi), sought out to photograph and interview. As if her skull weren't the one the regime's snipers dreamed of riddling with bullets. God, how incredible she was, unafraid of anything, with the same daring as the statue in the blind man's shop, when she used to pierce me with her laser gaze. Every moment held a thousand perils. She was like mercury: endlessly fluid and malleable, unimaginably swift.)

It was difficult, and not exactly enjoyable, to kiss a girl whose mouth was filled with qat. Her lips and tongue were obstructed by moist vegetation. We couldn't perform the usual two-tongued waltz we always found so deeply pleasurable. We had created our own language in the steps of this dance, capable of expressing everything we couldn't say in words, and heightened or mellowed at times by the sheer force of our passion. We listened to it closely, expanded on it earnestly, and developed it daily, with particular devotion.

What to do with the desire to kiss her that had overwhelmed me for months?

I was surprised by how fervently she wanted me from the moment we saw each other. She wanted me passionately, and in front of the mirror, too, specifically while chewing qat. She was acting like she'd just received a phone call from her husband, Imam Omar, ordering her to come home right away; as if she wanted to avenge herself on him like never before. It surprised me, this new symphony of vengeance, exactly a month after the revolution erupted.

She bent down towards my hips.

I was giddy with the tremulous sensation. It took me by surprise. A man who has never made love to a Salafi woman will never know how hard you can get (in a soft, warm lump of qat moistened with a houri's spit).

He'll never know how incredible that pleasure can be – a pleasure far greater than the traditional kind.

Tremendous pleasure – pleasures, rather. An abyss of divine pleasure. Two lavishly kohl-rimmed eyes, smiling self-confidently, laughing happily. She speaks to you with her eyes as she dances. She watches you, writhing with heathen lust. Your body incredulous, getting hard, stretching towards her, disappearing into her mouth…

She takes it in, lovingly, and moves it around in a soft, gooey mass. Undulating waves of qat soaked in her saliva.

You lock gazes in the mirror, her eyes brimming with the night. She watches you in the mirror, captive to the moment, and she watches herself, smiling. She sees how happy you are at seeing her so satisfied.

'Enjoy this for a long time… a long time… forever,' you can almost hear her say. 'The only thing that exists is this single, rebellious moment. Nothing else! In your last moments on earth, just before you meet the Reaper, this is where your thoughts will return.'

The only thing more beautiful than this bacchanalia was the ricochet of bullets twittering through the skies of Sana'a. There was a heady harmony at times between their roar and the rhythm of Hawiya's love.

Glory to revolutions!

Hawiya didn't pay any heed to the fact, dear Destroyer of Desires, that when I couldn't hold off any more, this would end with an explosion, gushing – warm, sticky, and pearlescent. Everything would get all mixed up in her mouth like everyone got mixed up with each other in Change Square.

Chaos, uprisings; she spluttered and nearly choked on the mass of qat as it was drenched in my fluids. Raging pleasure, like nothing else in the world. The electricity cut at the height of our frenzy and the bombing outside. Complete darkness. Then sex in the dark. Then sex by candlelight.

Sex during the revolution was a rebellious search for a way forward. A free-form dance that moved between darkness and candlelight, to the beat of bullets and far-off explosions.

Sex after the revolution was a world replete with surprises, difficult to describe.

The time we spent together after sex during these rehearsals for paradise also differed greatly from that before the revolution. Hawiya stayed for no more than fifty minutes; she had an appointment with a foreign radio journalist. And out of our fifty minutes together, she didn't spend more than ten with me. We spoke about the revolution, Change Square, and the future of the regime (in between a few deep kisses).

The other forty minutes she spent responding to important texts and a few urgent messages, commenting on Facebook, and sending sensitive emails.

We lay on the bed, naked and free as God made us. I watched her quick, charlatan's words that she tapped on the keyboard of her slim Mac in the candlelight. Her kohl-lined eyes scanned the screen. She rested her computer on her belly, just beneath the curve of her breasts.

Revolution, freedom, beauty, glory.

One of her calls seemed a bit strange to me, though. When her phone rang, she automatically withdrew to the other side of the room. Her voice changed slightly. She answered the call with a religious greeting: 'May God protect you and keep you, *habibi*.' (The ungendered version of the word 'you' she used bugged me. I didn't know if she was talking to a man, woman, or hermaphrodite).

Her religious colours hadn't faded completely.

The call seemed overly intimate. She said the word '*habibi*' a lot, more often than usual. Her voice became melodious, rich and tremulous in the way I loved. But she spoke more softly than usual.

I trained the full radar of my five or six senses on the tone of her voice. Her movements, her words, the light in her eyes.

Maybe she was speaking to one of her close proselytiser friends. The word *habibi* could be used for women too. She seemed particularly happy with the call.

She described her day's achievements with childlike joy; she clearly wanted to impress the caller.

Then, as someone who knew the language of her eyes, I noticed with horror: there was a glow of deep love there.

The end of her call was somewhat tense.

'I can't tell you right now. We'll talk later, *habibi*,' she said, before hanging up.

'You need an office to get this all done, *habibti*, and secretaries to respond to all these messages and calls,' I told her.

'In this country, if you want something done right, you have to do it yourself, *habibi*.'

'You need a team of guards, too.'

'No one protects anyone in this country, not even guards, *habibi*.'

'Then come with me to Paris, where it's safe and calm. Where we can be happy.'

She said nothing. It was like I was speaking gibberish, or a foreign language.

'I've got to go, *habibi*. I've got a really important appointment in the square. I'll see you tomorrow.'

She left the flat in a third veil, different to the one she'd been wearing when she stepped off the bus, and different to the one she had arrived at my flat in. It wasn't particularly shabby, yet neither was it stylish. It was rather agnostic – closer to 'the intermediate position', as the Mu'tazili phrase goes.

She took the first bus. I knew she would get off somewhere, and then take a private car to Change Square.

For me, dear Stealer of Spirits: 'Friday of Anger' was 'Friday of Sated Joy'. A Friday of sex, pleasure, wonder, and real revolution. A Friday of fantasies, romance, and life.

Glory to the revolutions, glory to anger!

Glory to life!

Chapter Eighteen

Post on the Facebook wall of my friend, M.G:

There is a small town with an army, police, citizens, a university, markets, courts, schools, streets, petrol stations, local restaurants, young lovers, obscure poets, pious ascetics, people parking their Peugeots together in the evening, elderly men recounting tales, barefoot children and mothers with asthma, workers coming from cement factories at dusk, Quran teachers who look like old Canaanites, and newspaper sellers who misplace a copy, or ten, of their papers every day.

Outside the city walls lurks a blind legion, awash with weapons, savage lust on their lips. They hover around the city gate like Vikings, amassing in the thousands, then vanishing in the blink of an eye. They use gunpowder savagely, without knowing why. They leave nothing behind but the hot ash of the fires they lit the night before. These fighters don't sleep; they carry torches ablaze, pointed towards the city. Dozens of miles away, they forge their proud ideals in the flames; they raise them on monstrous horns growing out of their foreheads.

This is a scene from long, long, long before the dawn of civilisation, long before the advent of writing. It can still be seen in Imran.

I woke up early the next morning, yearning to be in Change Square. I hurried to the bathroom to wash. For me, my morning shower has always been the most sacred moment of my day, and the most intimate. I can't start my day without it. I need hot water on my skull to stimulate the neurons in my brain, and wake me up. My circulatory system doesn't start working until my body is immersed in a stream of warm water. Without it, my brain can't put itself in order to begin the ballet of a new day.

I still haven't forgotten the morning in Paris I left the house without showering. I woke up late and almost missed an important meeting. By noon that day, I felt dizzy and tense, like I could barely breathe. I had to go all the way home, for my soothing, private ritual in the shower. Only after that could I return to the office and get on with my day as usual.

Here in Sana'a, there was no running water. The electricity, too, had cut out for several hours that night.

I could hear a news report on al-Jazeera from the bathroom. 'The ruling family's security forces attacked protesters in Change Square in Sana'a just after dawn prayer.'

The youth in the square called for help – they called on people to rush to defend the square.

I listened to the news in horror: the presidential guard and Saleh's thugs had been attempting to storm Change Square since dawn. They were attacking the protesters with tear gas, and other strange toxic gasses.

I emerged from the bathroom without having washed, breathless and ready to rush to the square. A heady, rebellious scent (hers, the most alluring perfume of them all) still danced on my body from the day before.

My body, and my delighted penis, still speckled with bits of her qat from the previous day.

Her qat, anointed with her sacred saliva.

Her saliva, which had mystically transformed my body into that of a god!

A brief interview with Hawiya on Al Arabiya channel.

I didn't care about the interview, but I felt reassured: glad to see that my Hawiya hadn't been harmed.

I listened to the interview while quickly getting dressed. She spoke about protest marches erupting all throughout Yemen in solidarity with the victims from Change Square.

I repeated traditional revolutionary maxims to myself, drafted by the old Marxist-Leninist propaganda and recruitment offices in my brain: *Aden and Sana'a are one heart, despite the Tyrant who revived sectarianism and discrimination to maintain his hold on power.*

I told myself confidently, naively: *All of Yemen is united against the ruling family today, more than ever before. There are Freedom Squares and Change Squares all over Yemen. When the gangsters in charge of the country fall, a new Yemen, the one I have long awaited, will finally be here!*

(If Khidr from Dhamar, who I'd met the day before in the square, had heard me, he would've burst out laughing. Just like how the employee responsible for scholarships in Aden in the seventies had laughed when I told him, in the coffee shop in the port of Sirah, that I'd rather have a grant to France, so I could see the sunset of capitalism with my own eyes, before spending the rest of my life building socialism.)

It was clear that this sweeping epidemic was incurable. This so-called disease that Yemen had contracted from its neighbours was an epidemic of freedom and dignity. It grew out of a desire for civil society and a different life, and would bring down the regime that spread only starvation and tyranny.

That much was clear, especially to eyes like mine that saw revolution everywhere, although it hadn't fully blossomed. I saw us leaping light years into the future, even if at the moment we seemed tethered to the spot, forced to watch the same men reshuffle power. Even if we seemed to be hurtling towards a bottomless abyss, towards even more chaos.

As I neared Change Square from the South, I joined the crowds that had come from all over to support the revolutionaries and sit-ins. It wasn't easy: the presidential guard and hired guards shot the brave people trying to join us.

The regime's thugs threw stones, and snipers were everywhere.

We tried to take cover in the backstreets, but were met with more thugs pelting us with stones.

Pure blue fear. My heart trembled. I used to love imagining revolutions. I thought they would be joyous, delightful festivals. I'd never imagined death, even though Death was always waiting in the shadows.

All night they kept trying to make us retreat, in an area between the Iranian health centre and Kentucky Round.

Dozens of people fell in front of me. People who couldn't run fast enough, people who couldn't breathe.

Thugs infiltrated the revolutionary ranks, and that made matters more complicated. The closer we got to the square, the more snipers we saw on the roofs.

I arrived at the commune just before midday. I'll never forget what I witnessed:

Crowds pouring in from every nook and cranny of the city, revolutionary songs being sung, celebrations everywhere, and so organised! (In a city that had never known order.) Ambulances transported the wounded to medical tents and field hospitals.

Our determination redoubled. Public sympathy with the revolution was clearly on the rise. Whole families arrived to join the sit-in in the square, men, women, and children.

A real revolution!

To reinvigorate our lives with the dreams we thought were scattered!

Glory to the revolution!

I'd walked into its open arms. My conviction swelled; I confidently asserted to someone that all of Yemen's previous 'revolutions' were no more than run-of-the-mill military coups.

I swear to you, dear Wrecker of Pleasures and Earthly Delights: more than once, I had to stop myself from crying in front of the crowds. (Najaa, if she were there, would have wept too.) I was so happy, watching people's solidarity as they waved pictures of 'martyrs of the revolution'.

People went out onto the streets, side by side. Seeing them released from their shackles was enough to fill me with joy, even if I didn't know exactly what the people *wanted*, where they were headed, or whether they even wanted *to want* in the first place.

I took refuge from the blazing sun in the tent of some tribesmen from near Sana'a. A small TV on the ground was showing the news on Al Jazeera. A few tribesmen were performing noon prayer while others watched TV. One showed us all shrapnel from last night: the regime's mercenaries' bullets, bomb shards, canisters of toxic gasses.

I filmed everything on my phone. I talked with everyone.

We listened to Al Jazeera together: the official spokesman of the regime denied the attack on the square.

'There was no blood. It was all makeup, just purplish-red Vimto syrup, that's all,' he said shamelessly, and a loyal official doctor confirmed it.

There was no limit to human beings' depravity, apparently.

We listened to testimonies by young people in the Square who had faced the regime's mercenaries. They described how security forces had prevented the residents of University City from coming into or out of the area. But they allowed thugs to fire guns and tear gas at the tents at dawn, and then escape over the wall of the university by the Square.

Shocking: three female civil society figures were there with us. None of the young men from the tribes seemed to mind being in the same tent with them. Something new was being born that day, rising up from the struggle like a phoenix from the flames.

How could they have minded? Female nurses were the first to tend to the wounded in the tents of Change Square, after all.

(They were everywhere. 'Like a fresh breeze, like birds from paradise,' one of the young tribesmen said.)

How could they have minded? Women and girls who lived near the square were the first to bring food to the revolutionaries as they arrived.

Something was being born here for the first time: new relations, new principles, new people.

A brief moment later, I realised I'd lost my phone in the hectic tents.

I was frustrated; all my family, friends, and acquaintances' numbers were saved in my phone, including my sister's home number, and the hotel phone number. I hadn't memorised them. Now my whole life in Yemen was lost forever.

I read the Fatiha over my phone in mourning and despondent defeat. I considered my phone a sacrifice to the God of Revolutions.

Then something happened that I'd never before experienced in Yemen: half an hour after I lost it (and also lost all hope of finding it), a tribesman came up to me. He was well dressed, and rather handsome.

'Pardon me, *ya ustaz*, we heard you lost your phone?' he said politely.

'Yes.'

'What kind is it?'

'An iPhone.'

'We found it near the door, maybe you dropped it there.'

'Thanks a million!' I paused. 'Could I ask what part of Yemen you're from?'

'The city of Imran, the Hashid tribe.'

My eponymous city, in my eponymous region, not far from Sana'a. A man from the same tribe as the President, the same tribes that shed Yemeni blood and looted the south after the 1994 Yemeni Civil War (may they pay on Judgment Day for their crimes against civilisation and history).

A new feeling swept over me. These revolutions were forging such a respectable, dignified world, one with the power to turn the dead into the living, and the living into the dead.

Then I remembered the philosopher from Dhamar with his round paunch, and what he had told me the previous day: 'Those people take after their fathers, who were Republicans in the morning and Monarchists in the evening... They're the biggest hypocrites in the world, just like their fathers and grandfathers before them. Don't believe them for a minute!'

The phrase *don't believe them* besieged me. It haunted me, provoked me, ruled my thoughts.

Back in the tent, I heard that tribes from around Sana'a had decided to come to protect the square from more attacks by the regime.

I began to worry: what if the revolution turned into an armed conflict or war, like in Libya? The revolution would be brought to its knees, tribes would be pushed to the sidelines, and those loyal in the military would reap the benefits.

The revolution would slip between the fingers of the youth in the squares. There would be a new balance of power, but it would be distributed between the same old powerful men, just like before.

Gaddafi's ghost and nightmares of the militarised Libyan revolution were resurrected in my mind. I remembered the terrible losses I'd suffered when he bombed Tripoli Street in Misrata, and the debts I would settle with the 'King of Kings of Africa' on Judgment Day.

Why did I think about military intervention? I don't know. But it turned out I wasn't far off the mark. Shortly afterwards, Al Jazeera broadcast a live interview with my arch rival, my 'brother-husband', Imam al-Hamdani (who was now more detestable than ever before), from his headquarters in Saudi Arabia, to which he'd fled. He condemned the security forces and the army for 'spilling Muslim blood' in the Square. He called on 'true Muslims in the army and security forces' to rebel against the President and join Change Square, to protect it from the ruling family's forces.

In other words: a direct call to militarise a peaceful revolution, and turn it into a war between two factions in a divided army.

I began to get rather nervous: a few military leaders arrived in Change Square that afternoon. They declared their solidarity with the revolution, and said they were prepared to defend it with force. Al Jazeera broadcast their statements from Change Square as they poured in.

It was nearly four in the afternoon.

Nearly the hour of our rehearsals for paradise. But I didn't expect my everlasting Hawiya, Queen of the Square, to come to my flat today. Not today.

Before going home, I paused in front of a tent showing videos of lectures that had been delivered in the square.

They were screening a lecture by Sheikh al-Zindani, head of Iman University. This was the man who had a patent on Quranic miracle drugs for treating not just cancer but AIDS too, and a recording of the Punishment of the Grave – the period following death but prior to the Day of Judgment, when souls of the unrighteous are punished. He had come to give a lecture in support of the revolution, on the official platform in the square.

Yes, dear Reaper: the most famous obscurantist of them all, here supporting the same revolution that I was.

(I hear my friend the Reaper chuckle lightly. 'An unsolvable equation,' he whispers to himself.)

In his lecture, he said that we needed to patent the revolution.

The word 'patent' didn't bode well, coming from his mouth. It meant that the revolution – just like his AIDS and cancer cures – was a sleight of hand.

I nearly exploded in anger: the revolutionaries were digging their own grave by recruiting an obscurantist. They may as well read the Fatiha over themselves.

There were people out there who must want me to hate the word *revolution* forever, I thought to myself. I, who once considered it the most noble, beautiful, and sacred word in the dictionary (alongside the words *sex* and *Najaa*, of course).

I fled from these 'patent-worthy' plots and schemes, back to my flat.

Hawiya arrived as usual. (For Salafi women, sex is a religious duty. It might be the only good thing about them!)

For her, our hours together were sacred, as was the revolution, as was I, as was Imam al-Hamdani. (She might've done better looking for a religion with three or four gods!)

Many tears over the martyrs that had fallen that day. Some of them were militants she'd been close to. She cried for them profusely, generously, and so did I, even though I was sure that some of them were the same people who vehemently insulted me over every secular post I wrote on Facebook.

The night was thick with bullets. Fear and anxiety. Quick, intense sex by candlelight, to the percussion of artillery shells rumbling in far-off parts of Sana'a. (I'd begun to love the sound.)

Then we talked about the horrors of this historic day, and all the little details.

Her two phones didn't stop ringing, texts didn't stop pouring in. (Change Square, all of Yemen, the whole world was in constant contact with her.)

She responded to some of them, in between kisses. She was affectionate with me in between emails. She was liberated from all restrictions here, and moved like a dancer, taking pride in her incredible body, naked like a houri in paradise. She paced from one side of the room to the other as she responded to comments or messages, in between quick kisses.

Revolution, arousal.

Then, again, one of her phone calls bothered me. I noticed that she lowered her voice, just like the day before. She went over to the other side of the room, again. Then the same light in her eyes as during yesterday's call, the same *May God protect you and keep you*, habibi. The same ambiguous *you* annoyed me all over again. The same outpouring of *habibi*s in practically every sentence.

Again, I trained my radar on the tone of her voice and the light in her eyes, as she whispered to whoever was on the other end. She lowered her voice for this call especially.

I realised they were talking about Imam al-Handani's interview on Al Jazeera, the one I'd heard before leaving Change Square. She seemed rather impressed with it. I wouldn't have expected that.

I watched her expressions intently in the dim candlelight. Her naked body, so sensual and lithe, stood in the corner of the room, so I couldn't hear what she was whispering.

I focused on the tone of her voice, with every neuron in my brain (all eighty-six to a hundred billion of them).

I noticed she was flustered as she ended the call, just like before.

'I can't tell you right now, we'll talk later,' she said hurriedly.

I remembered what she had once told me about the phrases that the two of them always used with each other. That she repeated: 'You're my only love, may God keep you and care for you,' three times, after he told her 'I love you by God and through God, I love no one but you, my only desire, my heart and soul, Ama al-Rahman,' three times.

Suddenly I realised who was on the other end of the line: Imam al-Hamdani himself.

The jealousy of a tiger, a thousand tigers, leapt into my whole being. A revolution inside a revolution exploded in my mind, without warning. My brain reached boiling point – the hundredth degree. ('Gradual changes lead to a paradigm shift.') Suddenly a shiver ran though my body, my words came out choked.

'Who were you speaking to?'

'Imam al-Hamdani.'

'You still love him, then?'

She hesitated. 'Why do you say that?' she asked, concerned.

'The light in your eyes, the number of times you called him *habibi*. I thought I was the only one you spoke to like that.'

'I don't remember using the word *habibi* once during the call.'

'That's even worse: when you call someone *habibi* unconsciously, and that many times, it's deeper, truer, more expressive, more significant. You still love him, don't you!'

'Yes. It's eternal love, just like I told you.'

'Why won't you just end the relationship?'

'What can I do? He won't have it!' She paused. Then with scarcely suppressed anger, revealed by a rare quiver of her eyelids, she added, 'Haven't I told you a hundred times: if you say his name one more time I'll leave you forever.'

Silence of the grave.

I didn't know what to say.

'Doesn't the split in the army after his speech on Al Jazeera worry you?' I asked without thinking. 'Doesn't it worry you that part of the army entered Change Square, and might soon take over the revolution?'

'On the contrary. Long live the army! Long live the army!'

Chapter Nineteen

Post on my Facebook wall:

Everyone who was part of Change Square knows the exact moment they smiled for the last time.

For many, it was the morning of 18 March 2011. The Friday of Dignity.

The massacre at dawn on 12 March was minor, a rehearsal compared to this. March 18 was tragically huge. Beyond belief.

In the hours before dawn, military snipers covertly stationed themselves on the roofs of all buildings around the square. Their objective: clear the square, and wipe out any protesters who wouldn't leave.

The result: dozens of dead, and hundreds of injured, all in just hours. Rivers of blood.

A pivotal moment in the revolution's history. There was before the Friday of Dignity, and there was after it.

Post on my Facebook wall:

After the Friday of Dignity began a long, long game, one ongoing still:

Three days after the massacre, a senior general defected from the President's army. (He was not so dissimilar to the President. They both had a close, longstanding relationship with the Salafis.) The general and his division defected to join the revolutionaries and protect the square.

The General had become a revolutionary! Most other 'revolutionaries' hailed his defection. They welcomed him and his soldiers, lifted them up on their shoulders, and chanted, 'Long live the army! Long live the army!'

Then several senior members of the former regime – the staunchest defenders of the ruling gang; by far the worst of the bunch – all followed suit. They too joined the revolution: long live, long live!

Then their leaders after that: long live, long live!

Finally, the real performance began, before an audience of people who had been robbed of their revolution:

The Gulf States' initiative to 'mitigate the Yemeni crisis.'

Immunity for the ousted president, his family, and members of his regime.

A third religious university. (The University of the Quran joined the ranks of two other Salafi universities, which had produced countless obscurantists and terrorists. In other words: two steps back and one step back. Forgive us, Vladimir Ilyich Ulyanov Lenin.)

The National Dialogue Conference. (Hypocritical theatrics which lasted eleven months in a five-star hotel. Six hundred participants paid in dollars).

In the end: 'No voice was louder than the National Dialogue Conference.' Just like the Yemeni Socialist Party in Aden in the seventies, 'whose voice rose above the rest.'

Oh, and I almost forgot: three days after the 'Friday of Dignity,' the General (a semi-literate man, a virtual copy of the ousted president) became President of the 'Yemeni Geniuses and Inventors Association.'

Long live the General, long live the General!

A summary of the charade:

The same old gang still held the reins of power, more firmly than ever before.

Yemen was still governed by the same zombies who'd been at the helm since I was a teenager. Now, nearly forty years later, they were the 'vanguard of the future.'

As a result:

The 'land of faith and wisdom' continued its descent into a bottomless abyss. Poverty, corruption, embezzlement, starvation, backwards obscurantist curricula, assassinations, chaos, sectarian war, deaths every day, child marriage, and the involvement of jihadis and al-Qaeda. As if creating the 'Islamic Emirate of Kandahar' was the final stage of 'Yemen's Democratic Revolution.' Forgive us again, Vladimir Ilyich Ulyanov Lenin.

Bye-bye, age of electricity, technology, civil society, and modern man.

Bye-bye, glimmer of hope.

Post on my Facebook wall:

I endlessly ruminate over my Arab bitterness.

Syria was ushered into the ranks.

Finally, a revolution I could get excited about, against one of the vilest of the dynastic dictatorial Arab regimes.

But this revolution, too, was betrayed. Its ranks filled with the same jihadis who destroyed my life. The same obscurantists who spilled the blood of my first love, and poisoned the mind of my second.

Daesh brazenly chopped the head off the only statue I'd ever upheld, and in his own home: Abul 'Ala al-Ma'arri. I'd hoped to see a thousand statues of him built before I died.

The revolution reeled, profusely bleeding, for years. A corpse factory. In comparison with Bashar al-Assad and his brutality (who may as well be gunning for a Nobel Prize in chemistry and engineering for so masterfully deploying barrel bombs), the Syrian revolution made Gaddafi (and all his barbaric crimes) look like Gandhi.

Post on my Facebook wall:

Bin Laden, the man who said, 'If the Yemeni Socialist Party survives, then I will not,' didn't survive.

But then again, neither did the Yemeni Socialist Party.

No one gets far in life (not even ruthless, avaricious criminals), except those who manufacture *ababil* for the modern age. Original *ababil*: birds that came down from heaven to protect Mecca from the Habashi army by dropping red clay bricks on

their elephants as they advanced on the city, according to
the Quran. Modern *ababil*: satellites, drones.

As for those happy to repeat the fairytales about *ababil* as
they plummeted down through all six heavens, or however
many there are supposed to be . . . they'll probably end up
in a cellar or cave. Or even the sewer.

Every person who was part of Change Square knows the exact moment when he smiled for the last time.

For me, it was six days before the Friday of Dignity:

The night of March 12;

In my flat;

In a dark silent moment.

In a shadowy, foul-smelling alley, sex, religion, power, and revolution had a fourway fuck.

Crying out, 'What can I do? He won't have it!' and 'Long live, long live!' That's what Hawiya and Imam al-Hamdani kept repeating. The Imam had called on the military to break from the regime and join the revolution.

Something inside me shattered after our conversation: it broke irreparably. Slowly, at the beginning. And then irreversibly.

That day, March 12, was also Najaa's birthday. (A strange coincidence; I didn't notice it at first.)

Let me tell you these dates again, dear Azazeel:

Exactly twenty years before the moment I heard Hawiya say: 'What can I do? He won't have it!' and 'Long live the army,' I was sitting with Najaa on a restaurant terrace in the Sinai.

Exactly thirty years before the moment I heard it, I was on a restaurant terrace on the island of Corsica.

Exactly sixteen years before that terrible moment, we were celebrating Najaa's last birthday, by the sea, on Imran Island in Aden, a few months before Najaa passed away...

I reflected on those precious days (I had become fixated on them, especially after our conversation on March 12). I realised that Hawiya and I would keep going around and around in this endless abyss. And that I needed to escape. I left early the next morning, heading towards Aden. I told my sister, Samia. (She'd tell Hawiya, I figured.)

It didn't matter.

I spent a week by the sea in Aden at the Gold Mohur Hotel. I wandered around by myself, and hiked up the high peaks of nearby mountains; up to the summit of Mount Shamsan, whose foothills reached all the way to the city. I remembered my mountain trips with Najaa, and everything we had said while staring out into the beautiful archipelago scattered all around us.

Our astounded gasps at the incredible view still echoed in my ears.

Long reflection. Blessed isolation.

I recalled the Aden of my childhood (when it was one of the most important ports in the world). It had been filled with people from India, Africa, and Europe, and all over Yemen too. A city of ships and sailors. Embracing all who fled from the pains of life.

According to mythology, there were undersea corridors linking Aden to India, along which jinn travelled. The city was an international capital in the making.

Arthur Rimbaud wished for death there in his final hours. Paul Nizan fled there when he was twenty and composed his famous text there, *Aden Arabie* (Sartre wrote a long introduction to it), before returning to France.

Despite all its pains and failures, Aden remained a beacon of hope for all who wanted to flee from the misery of the world and take refuge in a dream. Saadi Yousef's poetry still evokes Aden's loving haven, even from afar. It occupies the left half of the title of Muhammad al-Maghut's poetry collection: *East of Aden, West of God*. Mahmoud Darwish wandered the city streets, and praised it in verse and in person. He had an affinity with it, as did everyone who raises banners of freedom and revolution, or dreams of a new era in the Arab world.

Aden was throttled by gangs who met 'violence with violence' at the dawn of the seventies. It was shaken in January 1986 in the South Yemen Civil War. It was attacked by the vilest tribes and jihadi obscurantists in January 1994 in the Yemeni Civil War. They looted it savagely, crushing what remained of its civil society, refinement, and hope. They dealt the city a fatal blow.

I tried to sate my eyes with the beautiful view that unfurled itself between Shamsan Mountain and the sea. The incredible archipelago, charming natural protectorates. Flocks of migrating flamingos dancing on either side of the long sea road under a mighty sun that poured forth its light. I tried to let my last sorrows go.

A blazing beauty, nourishing the haemoglobin in my blood. My life depended on it.

'A beautiful view heals wounds,' a Chinese poet once said.

I felt like Aden's kith and kin. The city and I were one, so what could I do but breathe it in, moment by moment?

A trip to bid farewell to the port of Sirah. Another to Sheikh Othman. Dar Saad, al-Momadara, the ruins of Riverhemp. What ever happened to Doctor Dina, I often wondered. Who could tell me the rest of her life story, from the day she was kidnapped and unwillingly turned into a proletariat in the Fayoush Tomato Factory? (I knew the main details of her life until the day they took her – she'd told me them during our revolutionary Fridays together, the ones she didn't make me pay for.)

I left Aden three days after the Friday of Dignity, on March 21.

I returned to Paris trailing memories of defeat, like a Russian doll carrying lies within lies, all heavier than my feet could bear.

I was happy, like someone who had escaped from quicksand. And sad, at having lost Hawiya. Infinitely sad, at first. And then less and less so.

Eventually, I was no longer a prisoner to my grief over her life and her fate. Who knows, maybe Ama al-Rahman was happy the way things were.

Maybe I was no more than a passing tryst for her.

A desperate need to placate the roar of contradictions in her life (with more contradictions).

A way to avenge the heavy weight pressing down on that poor girl's delicate ribcage.

Who was I, really, compared to the great project of her life: 'rebuilding the caliphate state, our righteous forefathers' legacy, which they entrusted us to guard with our lives'?

I watched from afar as the Yemeni revolution floundered after the massacre on the Friday of Dignity.

What happened afterwards looked like a Punch and Judy show, starring the King of Flies, General of Flies, Imam of Flies, and Little Birds (the revolutionary youth).

The General and Imam of Flies regrouped, and joined together in Change Square. The scales were equally weighted: the General and Imam of Flies on one side, and the King of Flies and his family on the other.

The farce that was the Yemeni revolution ended like this:

A draw: 0 – 0. The King of Flies was on one side, and an alliance between the General and Imam of Flies was on the other.

The first side lost half its authority, and the second side gained half. But neither had it all.

The one who lost was that beautiful little bird: the dream of the Yemeni revolution. It fell flat on its beak, like a bird that tries to fly too soon. It plummeted straight down (long live the little bird, long live the little bird!) into the gaping maws of a three-headed beast: the King, General, and Imam.

When I returned to Aden, I deleted my Facebook account.

My life had arrived at a dead end. I felt ripe for death. I decided to live out my old age in peace. I was waiting for you, dear Breaker of Dreams and Worldly Desires, so I could divulge my pains and ask all these questions. I wanted to know the answers before I packed my bags and departed into the endless night on a ship you captain. The ship of the dead.

Before that, I had to settle accounts with another old dream of mine. I wanted to pursue it, this long-standing dream that had struck me off and on during life, one inspired by how passionate Najaa and I used to be about restaurants around the world. (All we needed to do was mention them, and we'd end up chatting about them for hours without noticing the time pass. We'd recall all the little details, and recall remembering them – usually while sitting in a restaurant. We had a special language, and our own private rituals, for talking about restaurants and food).

I finally realised this little dream.

At the end of September 2011, I was on the terrace of a restaurant in Paris, on the corner of a street in the 14th arrondissement, by the Alésia metro station. I ordered something simple: *shakshouka* with chorizo, the head chef's speciality. It was the first time I'd seen it on the menu. It sounded Spanish.

Men and women walked past, on that night full of passion and life. Summer was fading, and they looked like they were in the midst of the most joyous days of the year.

Abounding beauty, love flowing through the streets, passionate kisses, glittering lights. Suddenly I felt as sprightly as a dancer; dizzying vertigo; everything glowed; music, life, overflowing until death.

They were people enthralled with freedom, life, and love *en plein air*. Phrases like 'What can I do? He won't have it!' and 'Long live the army, long live the army!' were the last thing on their minds. (Even just remembering the words made me indescribably queasy.)

When I took the first bite of my meal, I realised that I'd eaten it before, in a previous life.

In that fabled, autumnal, Parisian air, it tasted as if it were my last supper. (I was slightly worried by how delicious I found it. It didn't seem natural.)

I wrote a short, rather personal article entitled 'The Last Supper' for a French weekly magazine. I described the dish and how I felt eating it; the restaurant, setting, and people around me. I provided an artistic critique of the dish, the restaurant's décor and music, and a description of the bartender and my interactions with him. In between bites, I let my cosmic, metaphysical reflections flow.

The magazine published it. People seemed quite impressed with it. Maybe the restaurant saw an increase in customers. Given the positive response to the article, the magazine asked me to turn it into a weekly column called 'The Last Supper', with the same spirit and structure. The paper contacted the restaurants, which invited me to come and order whatever dish I wanted, on the house, for my weekly column.

I was filled with a new professional passion, and a new desire.

Once a week (sometimes twice) I had the chance to reshape my thoughts, rearrange my failures, and summon memories of Najaa and the restaurants we went to together. I reflected on the abyss of my life, in blessed silence and solitude, and prepared my questions for you, dear Reaper.

As you may have noticed, I've asked a not-insubstantial number of them since I began with the phrase:

'Honestly, I don't understand anything. I'd be grateful, dear Reaper, if you'd help me grasp it all by explaining a thing or two. Surely, God has revealed to you the enigmas of creation and vicissitudes of fate.'

I prepared for these evenings out with an odd eagerness. I'd eat a full course meal in a corner of the restaurant, slowly and professionally, over two hours, or sometimes three. I silently observed the restaurant, the people, their expressions and conversations… and I remembered Najaa. I imagined what she would have said about everything I saw, heard, and tasted.

I wrote what she would have said. No more, no less.

She sent me her thoughts from the seventy-seventh heaven, the sky of ideas. Whenever I picked up the pen she gave me, I felt her with me. All I needed to do was hold it, and she whispered everything to me. She told me the words to pour down on the page, she who had turned our lives into a love story over stationary.

Every birthday she showered me with presents, and what she called 'side presents'. (I was crazy for these side presents, sometimes more than for the presents themselves.)

I was particularly fond of one of these side presents: a notebook of fine paper, a pen with fragrant ink, and a bundle of pencils, one for each year of my age.

For my first birthday in our shared home, she gave me twenty-one pencils. On my last birthday before she passed away, she gave me thirty-eight pencils. They were all beautiful. I don't know where or how she found them.

Those pencils were how I recognised Najaa (when the police summoned me to Saint-Michel station) among the other bodies ravaged and burnt in the bombing.

Dear Azazeel: when you see a queen among queens of the universe, a beauty queen, your only god, as no more than a body and blood mixed with a burnt fountain pen (the present), charred pencils, and scorched books (side presents), your life loses all meaning. It turns into a constant nightmare; it's plunged into darkness.

You realise that part of your mind has stopped working, forever. You realise that part of your life has collapsed, forever.

Aside from that, everything is idle chatter.

God, what goes on in the mind of a jihadi who puts a bomb in a metro station bin?

Pardon me, dear Reaper; you know *homo sapiens* better than anyone. This question has haunted me since I lost Najaa. This question will certainly be my last.

I was surprised that the King of the Dead looked so sad when I spoke about Najaa's body. I thought her passing would be just a grain of sand in the deserts of his kingdom.

I was also surprised by how eager he was to respond to that last question, before I finished my tale, as if the Angel of Endings would rather answer questions in reverse order, starting from the ending point.

'What was that jihadi thinking? He wished that all his bombs and IEDs could be replaced by one single bomb,' says my dear friend, unable to hide his rancour.

'Just one?' I respond, surprised.

'Yes, one very selective bomb. How efficient . . ?' muses my friend, vaguely and coldly. 'It would exterminate all the people who don't subscribe to his sectarian ideology. Billions of them, with just one explosion.' (In an instant, the weighty sorrows this damn man could have caused are heaved onto my shoulders.) 'He would have only spared the people he needed to keep manufacturing cars, phones, planes, medicine, and other products of the modern age that he and his kind can't live without. He also would've annihilated (without the slightest exception, this time) all museums, statues, paintings, and books – anything created by generations of humankind since the dawn of history who didn't ascribe to his ideology.'

My spine goes rigid as I listen to him. He understands this game of death and humankind better than anyone. Shivers. His soft, yet blunt words nearly splinter my ribs.

A long silence.

My friend notices that he's cut me off, and disrupted my train of thought.

'Go on, please,' he tells me. 'I'll answer your mishmash of questions all in one go, at the end.'

My 'Last Suppers' were moments of art and prayer, a way of clinging to what little I had left of life. Moments in which I fled from the everyday in the Arab world, news of massacres in Syria, images of missiles and aircraft raining massive barrel bombs and chemical explosives down on citizens. I fled from Yemen's revolution, that farce and fabrication; I fled from the 'land of total commotion and absolute stupidity,' as I had begun to call the Arab world.

I also began to take more and more of an interest in the 'land of absolute silence and total intelligence': China.

I became hooked after I read a book by the famous Chinese military strategist, Sun Tzu, *The Art of War.*

'The art of war is to defeat the enemy without confrontation, without the slightest loss, without shedding a drop of blood,' it says.

In other words: 'Before engaging in battle, victory must already be completely achieved.'

The way to do that: 'total intelligence.'

The concept was foreign to Arab civilisation, and to Western civilisation too. It was the complete opposite of the typical Arab sayings and idiotic Yemeni wisdom, like '*hanjama* (violent threats) are half the battle.' It blatantly contradicted Western culture, too: a culture of all-out war and self-aggrandising illegitimate assaults, from the Trojan War to the war that destroyed Iraq, and the two world wars in between. Yan Lio was a Chinese woman at the research centre where I work, and an old friend. This new world she described put me in a leg lock, just like Politzer's book had. (I was twenty years older than her, four times my own personal impassable 'Planck Era'.)

I felt a delicious sense of calm when we spoke about things other than our research. Her mind was free of all our culture's shackles. For her, everything in life was a Chinese-style war, including our relationship and conversations, and even her relationship with herself. (In other words: jihad of the self, the greatest jihad. 'The struggle against the evil of one's own soul,' as the sage prophetic saying goes.)

Speaking with her was an endless breath of fresh air.

She knew nothing about metaphysics – that weight that choked our lives and made it impossible for us to breathe – and I was glad.

All our 'knowledge imparted by God', the list of our fanatics and forbidden apples, prayers for rain and prayers for snow, fatwas from fiqh jurists – these were concepts she paid no mind, just like a billion other Chinese people.

Yan Lio couldn't understand these concepts and fairytales any more than I could understand the croaking of frogs.

She heard only Huainanzi:

Leap from nothingness into being
From being into nothingness
With no end or beginning
No one knows where a flower will grow

Yan Lio looked at our clash of civilisations, our cultures in the East and West, steeped in religion, just like a lioness might look down from a mountaintop at two wolves fighting in the valley below.

I realised this while we were sitting in a café outside a literary conference in Aberdeen, Scotland, leafing through a few French, Arabic, and Chinese newspapers.

Yan Lio was reading a French article looking back on the killing of Bin Laden. She looked at a photograph that had appeared in most newspapers a few days after he was killed in May 2011.

In the image: over twenty American soldiers and civilians. Obama sat among them. They were all watching a huge screen, which was streaming the attack operation on Bin Laden's house in Pakistan live, to a modern, luxurious operations room somewhere in America.

I noticed a sly, beautiful smile on Yan Lio's lips as she looked at the photo.

This Chinese woman of mine was taken by the image. Its composition followed the spirit of the *Art of War*.

'This photograph is so clever because it makes us look at the faces of the people observing,' she told me. 'The focal point is intriguing; the way it's been staged is ingenious. We look to where they're directing their gaze – at the screen. But in the photo, we can't see what's happening on the screen! The invisible is more important than the visible: that is the philosophy of the *Art of War*. We know it means that what's happening on the screen is horrible. Really horrible. You imagine it as best you can, but you know it's worse than you could imagine.'

Her ruminations made an impression on me as I stared at the image. I felt very far away.

My mind's eye filled with bodies after the metro bombing: the most horrific image of all. I didn't need to imagine any more than that – thanks Yan Lio.

I scratched my head. This was how capitalism, which refused to set, was rising. It would triumph, just as death always triumphs in the end.

Yan Lio read an article in a Chinese newspaper: *Israel celebrates the launch of the new Horizon 10 Satellite, to spy on dining room tables and bedrooms in the Middle East.*

I was leafing through an Arabic newspaper, and paused to read an article unrelated to space, or even the earth itself (where we still haven't solved existential questions like whether women should be allowed to drive). I didn't dare translate it for Yan Lio. It concerned a field we Arabs have a monopoly on: the science of 'Punishment of the Grave'.

The article described a few important discoveries our scientists had made in the field. It summarised a lecture made by the President of Iman University in Yemen, a member of the former Presidential Council (the one who had been asked by the 'revolutionaries of Change Square' to grant them a patent). In the video, he showed a tape that his assistant had recorded along the Russian-Norwegian border of a million voices screaming during Punishment of the Grave. He claimed that you could tell which were men's voices and which were women.

There was another discovery related to Punishment of the Grave: what colour 'snakes and scorpions deep in the earth' are, and how many limbs and heads they have.

Another discovery: how graves expand and shine like the moon during 'Comfort of the Grave'.

'What are you reading? What's the matter?' Yan Lio asked me.

'Nothing, nothing . . .'

'Are you sure?'

'Quite sure!'

'Quite?'

'Yes!'

'At the end of the twentieth century, the Americans asked us to radically change our economic and political system,' Yan Lio said. 'We said "No." Economy: yang. Politics: yin. One influences the other, bringing them both into harmony. You can't change yin and yang at the same time; that will result in collapse. What happened later with the Soviet Union proved that. So we changed the economy, and became more capitalist than the West. But we preserved the dictatorial communist political system that governs our everyday lives. We developed a Chinese concept the West will never understand: a socialist market economy!'

I scratched my head again. I'd arrived in France hoping to see the sunset of capitalism, and instead saw it rising higher and brighter.

Yan Lio didn't need to tell me what everyone else knew:

The Chinese economy was superior. It was based on total intelligence and absolute silence, and would soon dominate the world. (Yan Lio herself wasn't arrogant, and didn't ever make a fuss. She was 'like a ghost that leaves no trace, like water that no one can mar,' as Huainanzi said).

I spent a wonderful week with her in Aberdeen.

We drove around the North Seas shores, and whiskey distilleries in the Scottish countryside. We bought delicious, expensive spiced varieties with a rare peppery aroma.

We chatted for hours (she was good natured, ethereal) in an unusually named café in the heart of the city: the Soul Café. Years earlier it had been part of the Gilcomston Church.

This Chinese woman of mine didn't seem to understand why I was so shocked at seeing a church turned into a bar.

Perhaps it was all the same thing, in her eyes, so bright and always laughing. As if somehow the bar were a church and the church were a bar. Yin and yang. Two sides of a single human social need.

These days, I begin my mornings by reading Chinese newspapers in translation. I listen to radio and television stations from Shanghai. Then I read translations of Chinese classics.

Some daily Chinese wisdom:

'He who can masterfully open and close the channels of the soul becomes like the tao: so infinitely small nothing can penetrate it, so infinitely large nothing can contain it.'

I've started to learn how to read and write Chinese too, with more enthusiasm than I'd ever had for anything.

I dream of being able to write this Chinese maxim in its original language:

'He who triumphs through another's designs possesses true divine artistry.'

My next step: to visit Shanghai with Yan Lio.

A little dream I hope to make come true on the trip: riding a bicycle with a huge mass of Chinese people all headed to work early in the morning.

Yan Lio and I have a weekly routine: an hour of swimming, followed by an hour running in the woods. Then we spend two hours massaging each other any way we like. I call it 'yin-yang chemistry.'

'Before arriving in Shanghai, we'll have a layover in Mozambique,' I told Yan Lio. 'I've dreamed of going there for ages. I don't want to depart this life before settling my accounts with the country.'

I wanted to know where exactly Mozambique was, and what had happened to the revolution we once debated until four in the morning. I thought of the First Party Conference for the Sheikh Othman and Surrounding Neighbourhoods Branch, and the resolution we drafted to support them, back in the early seventies.

After Mozambique I wanted us to spend two or three days on the beaches of Imran Island near Aden. If I don't go swimming there at least once a year, I feel cold and choked for the rest of the year. (I was a believer, just like Najaa, that, 'Time alone is our demise, in the sea alone are we revitalised.)

Even today, I couldn't believe that the three of us had never swum in it together. (Yan Lio was pregnant, in her fifth month). The three of us: the Imran family.

(Did I just say, 'the Imran family'? Even today, I didn't know whether Imran was supposed to be Moses' father, or Aaron's, or maybe Mary's? It doesn't matter.)

I love my Hebrew-Arabic name; *ebry-araby*, as we'd say in Arabic. The Arabic words for Hebrew and Arabic are intriguing, so similar – the only real difference is switching around the 'b' and the 'r', and yet . . .

I love it a lot. I love the names Aaron and Mary too. And the name Gao, like Gao Xingjian, author of *Soul Mountain,* which won the Nobel Prize for Literature.

Then, who knows, maybe in Aden I'll find my true companion, the last other rebel in the world. We can chant my favourite verse together in the streets: *The people want to bring down the regime!* Even if the people don't really *want* things anymore.

It would be enough for him just to be alive. And if he were still engaged in the fight, it would be a dream come true, one only the poets and half-mad still believe in.

Yan Lio changed our travel plans. (She doesn't need a wristwatch; like all Chinese, she can 'read time in a cat's eye'. Maybe she can read maps in a mouse's eye, too.) She massaged me sensually during our two hours of yin-yang alchemy, and then finished me off by really getting my blood flowing.

My Chinese woman didn't change our travel plans because she was five months pregnant, or out of a specific desire. She simply mentioned these two Chinese maxims:

'There's nothing harder than searching for a black cat on a dark night. Especially if there's no cat in the first place.'

And: 'A true traveller sets forth without a map.'

Glossary

abaya: a voluminous black garment worn over other clothes by some Muslim women when in public.

Ababil: birds, with the world's largest wings, said in the Quran to have come down from heaven to protect Mecca from the Habashi army by dropping red clay bricks on their elephants as they advanced on the city.

duha and *witr*: one of the optional additional prayers that can be made at specific times in between the five obligatory daily prayers in Islam.

Fatiha: the opening Sura, or chapter, of the Quran, used as a blessing for many situations or activities, and always read over the dead.

Praise be to God, Lord of the Worlds:
Merciful to all,
Compassionate to each!
Lord of the Day of Judgement.
It is You we worship, and upon You we call for help.
Guide us to the straight path,
The path of those upon whom Your grace abounds,
Not those upon whom anger falls,

Nor those who are lost.

fiqh: Islamic jurisprudence — the human attempt to understand the divine law known as Sharia.

habibi, habibti (male and female versions of the noun): an endearment, used both platonically and romantically. The term can therefore be correctly translated as 'my darling, my sweetheart', as well as 'mate, pal', depending on the user and context.

hayati: a romantic endearment, literally 'my life'.

hijab: a scarf or piece of cloth that covers the hair and neck but not the face, and can be wrapped in a wide variety of styles including, in some regions, so as to reveal a section of hair around the fringe area. Worn by many but by no means all Muslim women around the world, its use is based on a Quranic verse mentioning women covering (or 'beating') their 'angles' or 'pockets', the interpretation of which is strongly contested.

houri: beautiful young female virgins said to await the Muslim faithful in paradise.

Houthis: a Shia-led religious-political movement that emerged in the 1990s and began an on-and-off fight against the government of then-president Ali Abdullah Saleh in 2004. In late 2014, Houthis fixed their relationship with the ousted president and with his help they took control of Sana'a and much of northern Yemen.

jinn: a supernatural spirit appearing in pre-Islamic Arabian mythology as well as the Quran; of a lower rank than the angels, jinns are able to appear in human and animal forms, and to possess humans.

Kaaba: the most holy site in Islam, towards which Muslims around the world face when praying. Located in the centre of the Great Mosque in Mecca, the Kaaba is an ancient square stone building on the site of multiple pre-Islamic shrines perhaps going back to those built by Adam and Eve. The sacred Black Stone set in its south-eastern corner is said to be the only remnant of the original shrine built on the spot by Abraham.

Mahdi: the prophesied redeemer of Islam referred to in the Hadith (sayings of the Prophet Mohammed) and seen differently by Sunni and Shia Muslims. Islamic traditional is that the Mahdi's rule will coincide with the second coming of Jesus Christ.

miswak: a traditional medicinal teeth-cleaning stick mentioned in the Hadith (sayings of the Prophet Mohammed). Used widely across Muslim areas of Africa and in the Arabian Peninsula, Central Asia, the Indian subcontinent and South East Asia, it comes from the Salvadora persica tree.

mujahideen: Islamic guerrilla fighters or Holy Warriors engaged in jihad (plural form of the noun mujahid).

niqab: a face veil revealing only the eyes, worn in conjunction with the hijab by some Muslim women.

omri: a romantic endearment, literally 'my life'.

qalbi: a romantic endearment, literally 'my heart'.

qat: The leaves of the flowering shrub Catha edulis, native to the Arabian Peninsula and the Horn of Africa. Chewing qat is a long-established social custom in (mainly male) communities all around the Red Sea. It contains cathinone, an amphetamine-like stimulant, which is said to cause excitement, loss of appetite and euphoria.

rakaat (singular *rakat*): a single round of prayer, including all the prescribed words and movements. Different numbers of *rakaat* make up the full set of prayers at the various times of day.

sheikh, sheikha: term of respect for an elder or a religious authority (male and female form of the noun).

Sunnah: the habits of the Prophet Mohammed, as recorded by those who knew him. The Sunnah are a crucial element of Islamic practice.

a Sura: a single chapter of the Quran.

Takfiri: A Muslim who declares another Muslim an apostate and therefore no longer a Muslim.

tashahhud: part of the prayer, differing slightly in various traditions of Islam, but usually containing a formulaic greeting to God and the Prophet, and the profession of Muslim faith in a single God with Mohammed as his only messenger.

Ummah: a global supra-national 'nation' of Muslim believers, a united global family of Muslims.

wahji: a romantic endearment, literally 'my flame'.

ya Haj: a respectful form of address, in the male form, implying that the person spoken to has performed the pilgrimage to Mecca, the Haj.

ya ibni: literally 'my son', an affectionate or familiar form of address to a younger man.

ya ustaz: a respectful form of address, in the male form, implying that the person spoken to is wise, intelligent, or right (literally 'teacher').